3 4028 09315 0416
HARRIS COUNTY PUBLIC LIBRARY

J 741.594 Bek
Beka
Dance class. 3, African
    folk dance fever

$10.99
ocn779265131

D1275484

Dance Class

Crip • Art

Béka • Story

Maëla Cosson • Color

New York

Dance Class Graphic Novels Available from PAPERCUTZ™

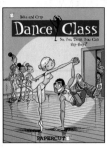

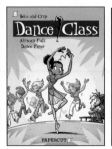

#1 "So, You Think
You Can Hip-Hop?"

#2 "Romeos and
Juliet"

#3 "African Folk
Dance Fever"

#4 "A Funny
Thing
Happened on the
Way to Paris..."

#5 "To Russia,
With Love"

#6 "A Merry Olde
Christmas"

#7 "School Night
Fever"

#8 "Snow White and
the Seven Dwarves'"

DANCE CLASS graphic novels are available for $10.99 only in hardcover, available from booksellers everywhere. You may also order online from Papercutz.com. Or call 1-800-886-1223, Monday through Friday, 9 - 5 EST. MC, Visa, and AmEx accepted. To order by mail, please add $4.00 for postage and handling for first book ordered, $1.00 for each additional book and make check payable to NBM Publishing. Send to: Papercutz, 160 Broadway, Suite 700, East Wing, New York, NY 10038.

DANCE CLASS graphic novels are also available digitally wherever e-books are sold.

Papercutz.com

DANCE CLASS #3
"African Folk Dance Fever"
Studio Danse [Dance Class], by Béka & Crip
© 2009 BAMBOO ÉDITION.
www.bamboo.fr

Béka - Writer
Crip - Artist
Maëla Cosson - Colorist
Joe Johnson - Translation
Tom Orzechowski - Lettering
Adam Grano - Production
Beth Scorzato - Production Coordinator
Michael Petranek - Associate Editor
Jim Salicrup
Editor-in-Chief

ISBN: 978-1-59707-363-9

Printed in China
September 2014 by WKT Co. Ltd.
3/F Phase I Leader Industrial Centre
188 Texaco Road, Tseun Wan, N.T.
Hong Kong

Distributed by Macmillan
Second Papercutz Printing

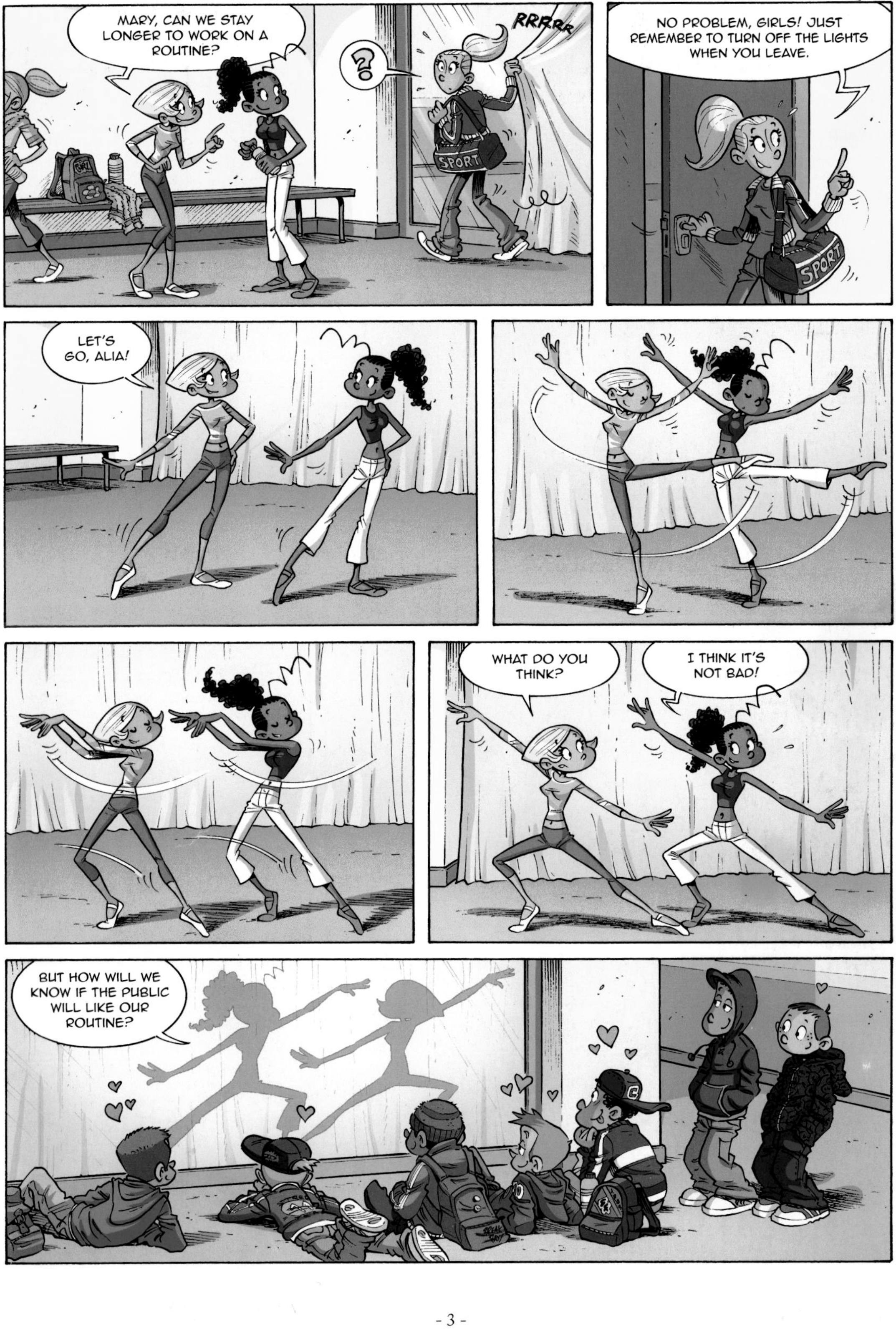
MARY, CAN WE STAY LONGER TO WORK ON A ROUTINE?
RRRRR
?
SPORT
NO PROBLEM, GIRLS! JUST REMEMBER TO TURN OFF THE LIGHTS WHEN YOU LEAVE.
SPORT
LET'S GO, ALIA!
WHAT DO YOU THINK?
I THINK IT'S NOT BAD!
BUT HOW WILL WE KNOW IF THE PUBLIC WILL LIKE OUR ROUTINE?

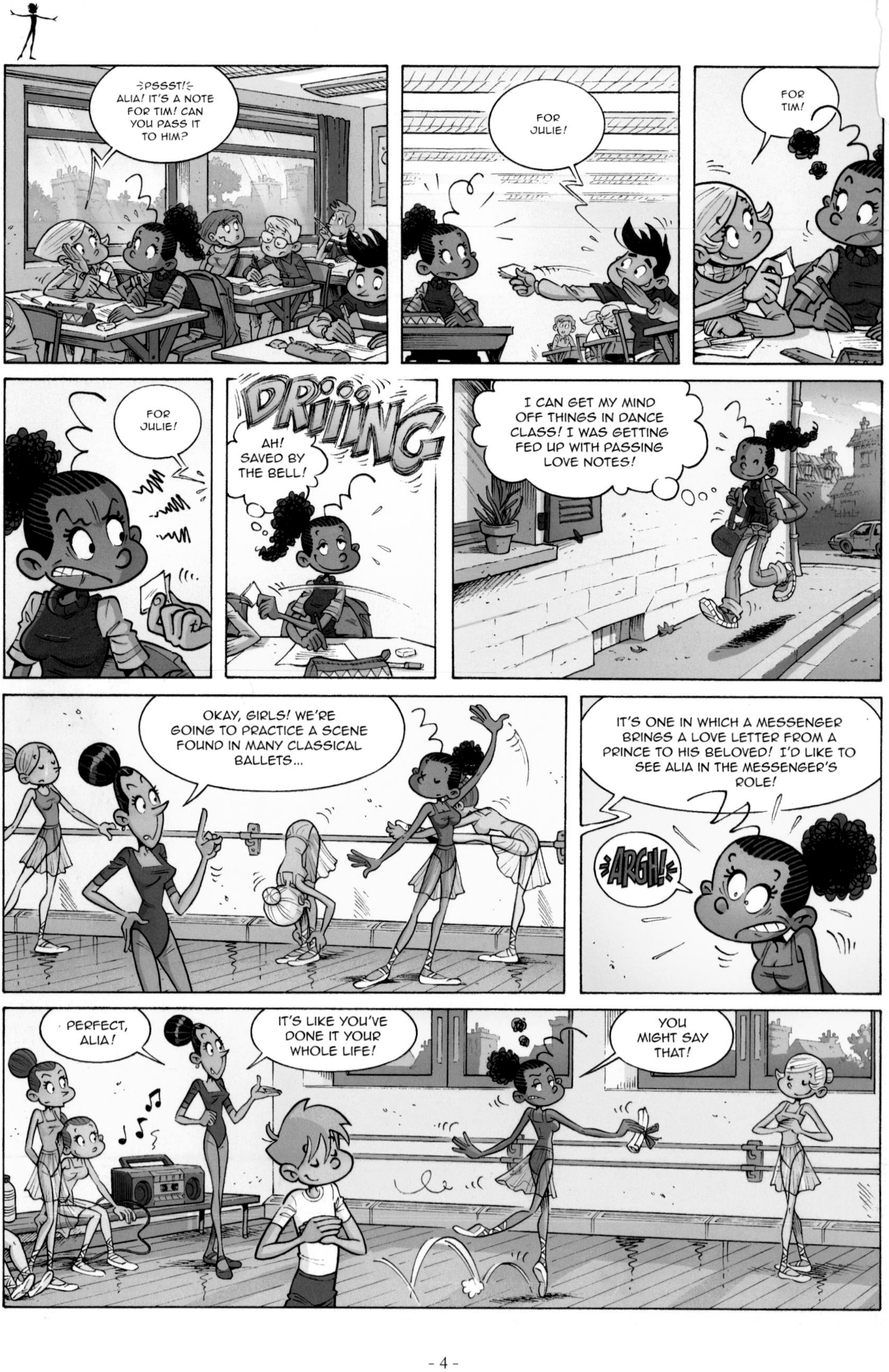
PSSST! ALIA! IT'S A NOTE FOR TIM! CAN YOU PASS IT TO HIM?
FOR JULIE!
FOR TIM!
FOR JULIE!
DRIIING
AH! SAVED BY THE BELL!
I CAN GET MY MIND OFF THINGS IN DANCE CLASS! I WAS GETTING FED UP WITH PASSING LOVE NOTES!
OKAY, GIRLS! WE'RE GOING TO PRACTICE A SCENE FOUND IN MANY CLASSICAL BALLETS...
IT'S ONE IN WHICH A MESSENGER BRINGS A LOVE LETTER FROM A PRINCE TO HIS BELOVED! I'D LIKE TO SEE ALIA IN THE MESSENGER'S ROLE!
ARGH!
PERFECT, ALIA!
IT'S LIKE YOU'VE DONE IT YOUR WHOLE LIFE!
YOU MIGHT SAY THAT!

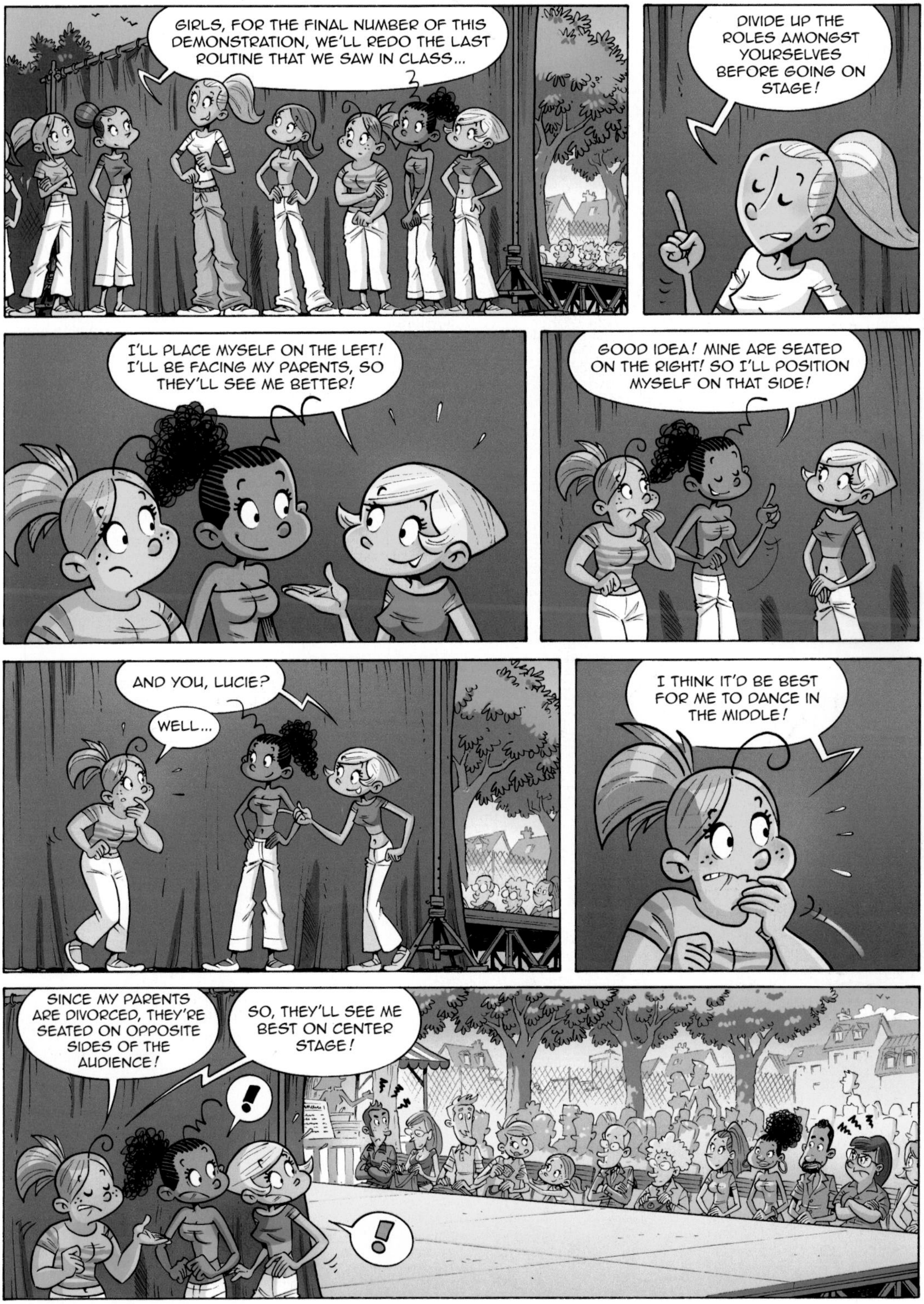
GIRLS, FOR THE FINAL NUMBER OF THIS DEMONSTRATION, WE'LL REDO THE LAST ROUTINE THAT WE SAW IN CLASS...
DIVIDE UP THE ROLES AMONGST YOURSELVES BEFORE GOING ON STAGE!
I'LL PLACE MYSELF ON THE LEFT! I'LL BE FACING MY PARENTS, SO THEY'LL SEE ME BETTER!
GOOD IDEA! MINE ARE SEATED ON THE RIGHT! SO I'LL POSITION MYSELF ON THAT SIDE!
AND YOU, LUCIE?
WELL...
I THINK IT'D BE BEST FOR ME TO DANCE IN THE MIDDLE!
SINCE MY PARENTS ARE DIVORCED, THEY'RE SEATED ON OPPOSITE SIDES OF THE AUDIENCE!
SO, THEY'LL SEE ME BEST ON CENTER STAGE!
!
!

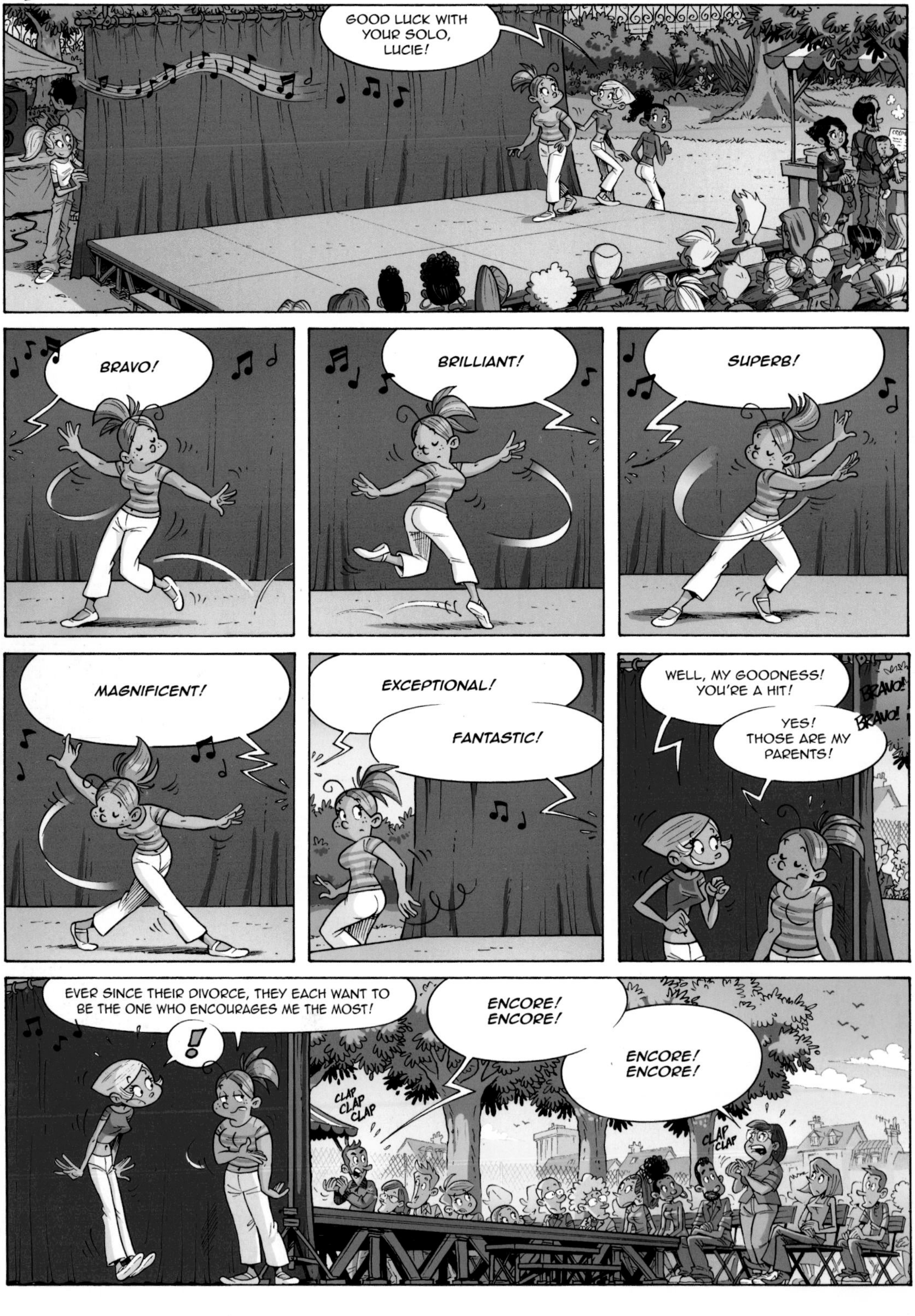
GOOD LUCK WITH YOUR SOLO, LUCIE!
BRAVO!
BRILLIANT!
SUPERB!
MAGNIFICENT!
EXCEPTIONAL!
FANTASTIC!
WELL, MY GOODNESS! YOU'RE A HIT!
YES! THOSE ARE MY PARENTS!
BRAVO!
BRAVO!
EVER SINCE THEIR DIVORCE, THEY EACH WANT TO BE THE ONE WHO ENCOURAGES ME THE MOST!
!
ENCORE! ENCORE!
ENCORE! ENCORE!
CLAP CLAP CLAP
CLAP CLAP

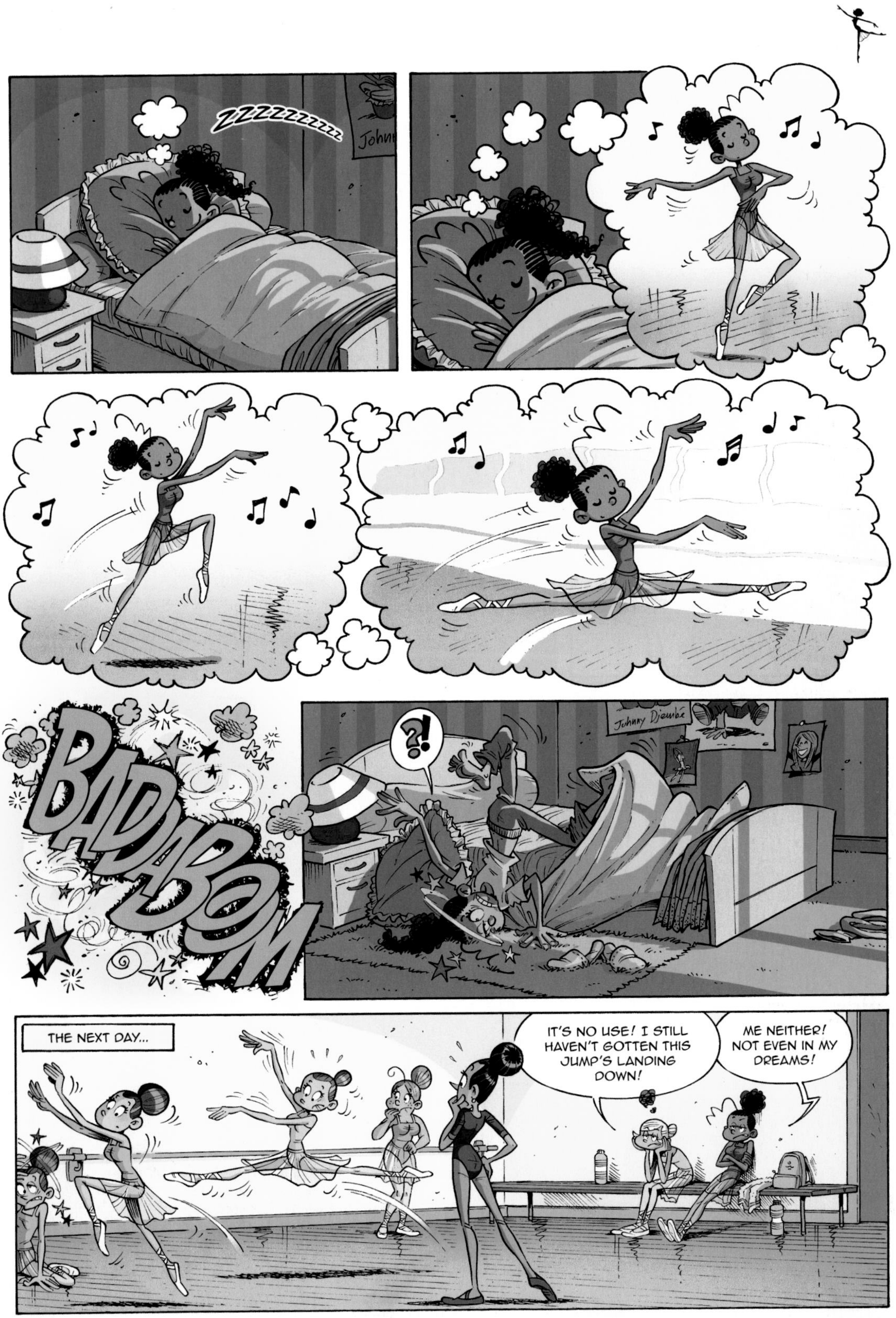
ZZZZZZZZZZZ
Johnny
BADABOOM
?!
Johnny Djumbé
THE NEXT DAY...
IT'S NO USE! I STILL HAVEN'T GOTTEN THIS JUMP'S LANDING DOWN!
ME NEITHER! NOT EVEN IN MY DREAMS!

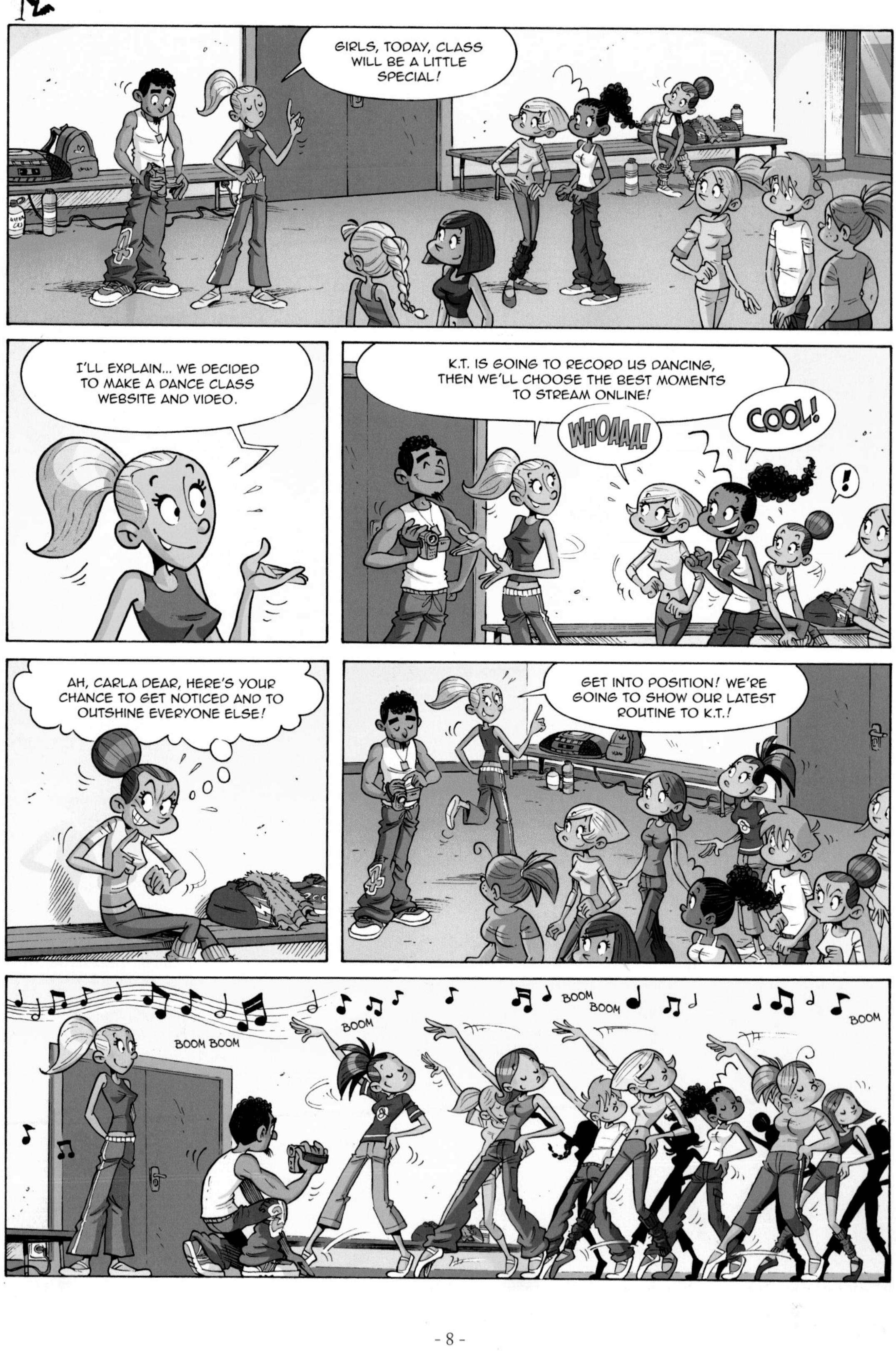

GIRLS, TODAY, CLASS WILL BE A LITTLE SPECIAL!
I'LL EXPLAIN... WE DECIDED TO MAKE A DANCE CLASS WEBSITE AND VIDEO.
K.T. IS GOING TO RECORD US DANCING, THEN WE'LL CHOOSE THE BEST MOMENTS TO STREAM ONLINE!
WHOAAA!
COOL!
!
AH, CARLA DEAR, HERE'S YOUR CHANCE TO GET NOTICED AND TO OUTSHINE EVERYONE ELSE!
GET INTO POSITION! WE'RE GOING TO SHOW OUR LATEST ROUTINE TO K.T.!
BOOM BOOM
BOOM
BOOM
BOOM
BOOM

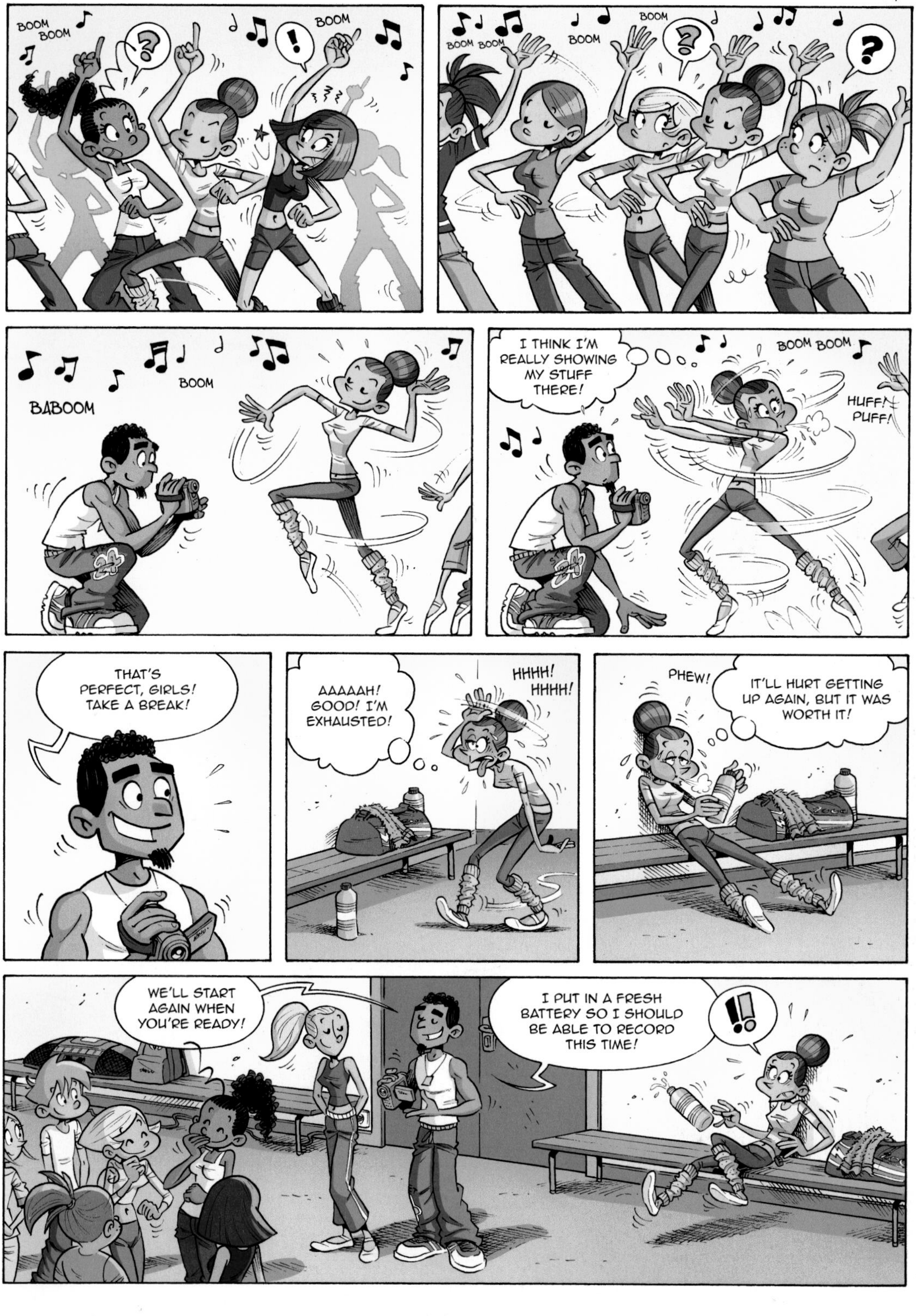
BOOM BOOM
BOOM
BOOM
BOOM BOOM
BOOM
BABOOM
BOOM
I THINK I'M REALLY SHOWING MY STUFF THERE!
BOOM BOOM
HUFF! PUFF!
THAT'S PERFECT, GIRLS! TAKE A BREAK!
AAAAAH! GOOD! I'M EXHAUSTED!
HHHH! HHHH!
PHEW!
IT'LL HURT GETTING UP AGAIN, BUT IT WAS WORTH IT!
WE'LL START AGAIN WHEN YOU'RE READY!
I PUT IN A FRESH BATTERY SO I SHOULD BE ABLE TO RECORD THIS TIME!

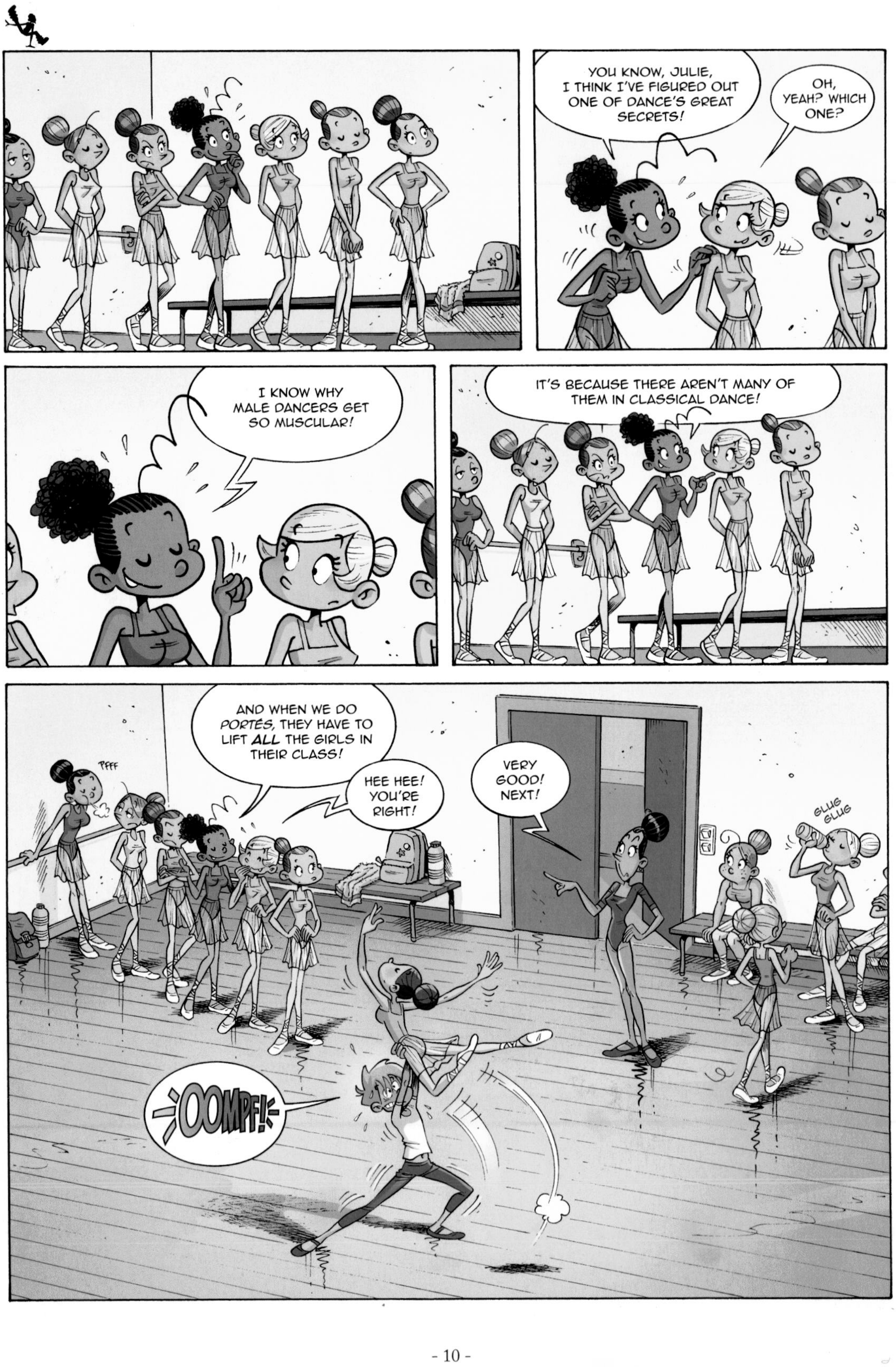
YOU KNOW, JULIE, I THINK I'VE FIGURED OUT ONE OF DANCE'S GREAT SECRETS!
OH, YEAH? WHICH ONE?
I KNOW WHY MALE DANCERS GET SO MUSCULAR!
IT'S BECAUSE THERE AREN'T MANY OF THEM IN CLASSICAL DANCE!
AND WHEN WE DO PORTÉS, THEY HAVE TO LIFT ALL THE GIRLS IN THEIR CLASS!
PFFF
HEE HEE! YOU'RE RIGHT!
VERY GOOD! NEXT!
GLUG GLUG
OOMPF!

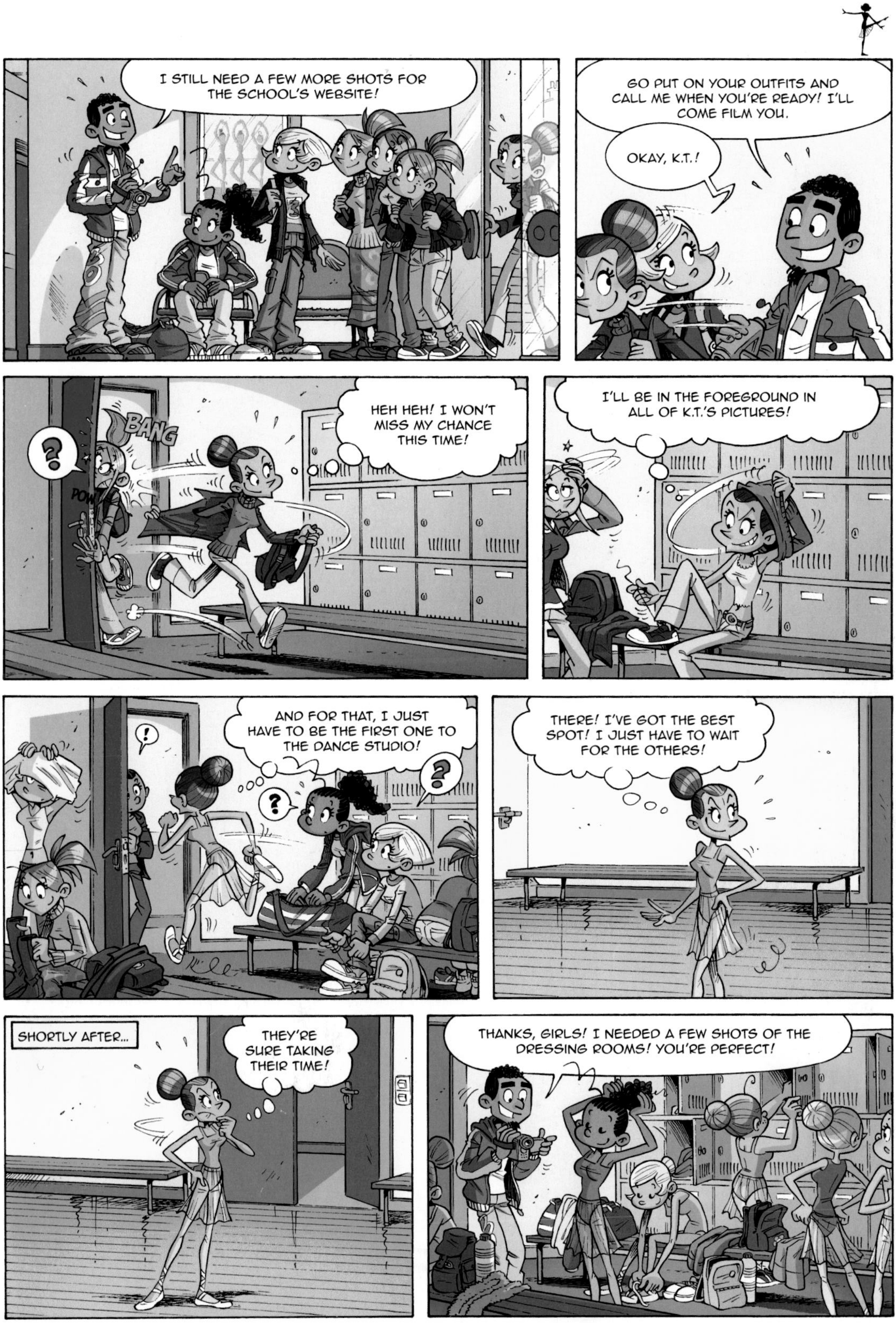
I STILL NEED A FEW MORE SHOTS FOR THE SCHOOL'S WEBSITE!
GO PUT ON YOUR OUTFITS AND CALL ME WHEN YOU'RE READY! I'LL COME FILM YOU.
OKAY, K.T.!
?
BANG
POW
HEH HEH! I WON'T MISS MY CHANCE THIS TIME!
I'LL BE IN THE FOREGROUND IN ALL OF K.T.'S PICTURES!
!
AND FOR THAT, I JUST HAVE TO BE THE FIRST ONE TO THE DANCE STUDIO!
?
?
THERE! I'VE GOT THE BEST SPOT! I JUST HAVE TO WAIT FOR THE OTHERS!
SHORTLY AFTER...
THEY'RE SURE TAKING THEIR TIME!
THANKS, GIRLS! I NEEDED A FEW SHOTS OF THE DRESSING ROOMS! YOU'RE PERFECT!

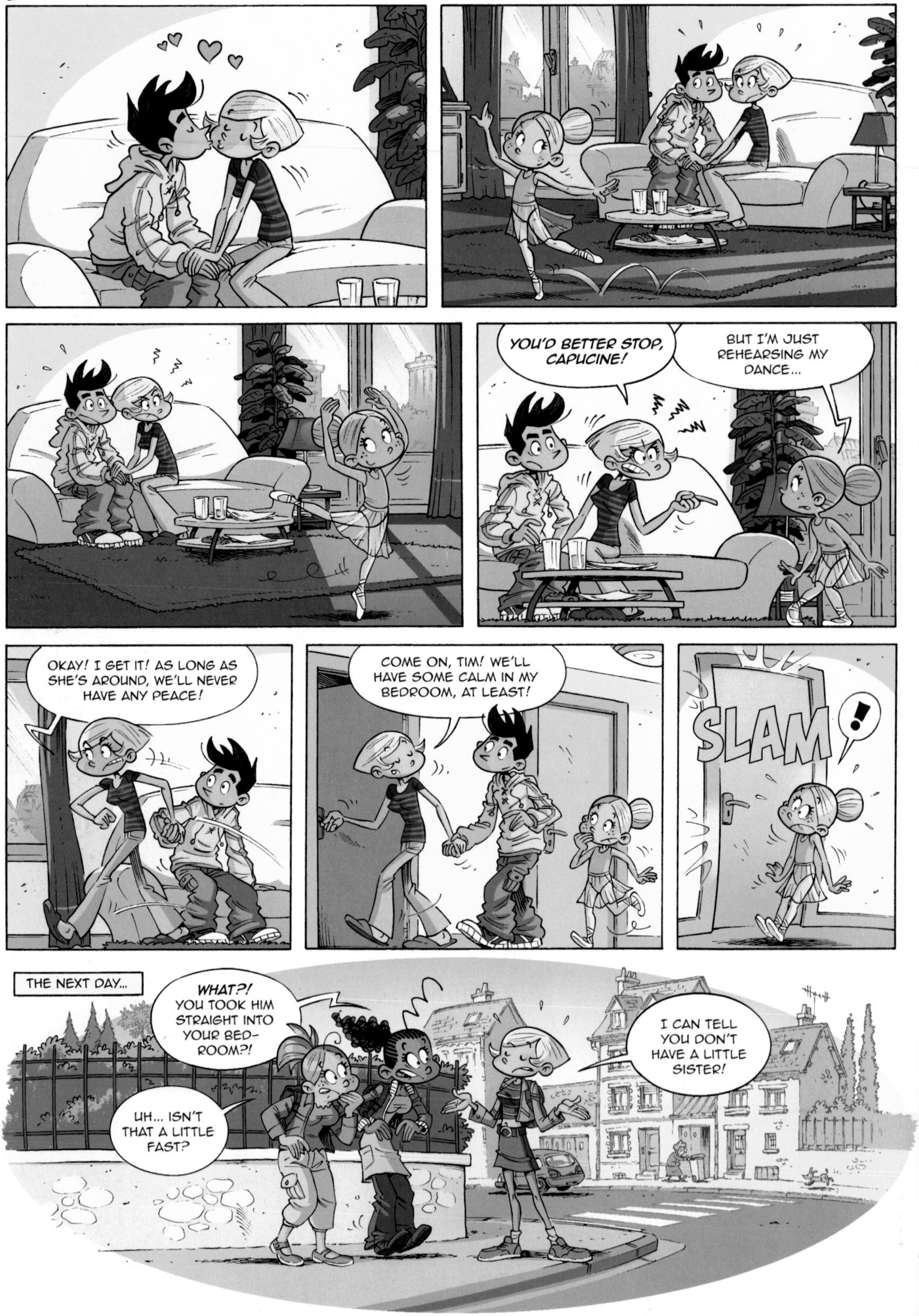
YOU'D BETTER STOP, CAPUCINE!
BUT I'M JUST REHEARSING MY DANCE...
OKAY! I GET IT! AS LONG AS SHE'S AROUND, WE'LL NEVER HAVE ANY PEACE!
COME ON, TIM! WE'LL HAVE SOME CALM IN MY BEDROOM, AT LEAST!
SLAM
!
THE NEXT DAY...
WHAT?! YOU TOOK HIM STRAIGHT INTO YOUR BED-ROOM?!
UH... ISN'T THAT A LITTLE FAST?
I CAN TELL YOU DON'T HAVE A LITTLE SISTER!

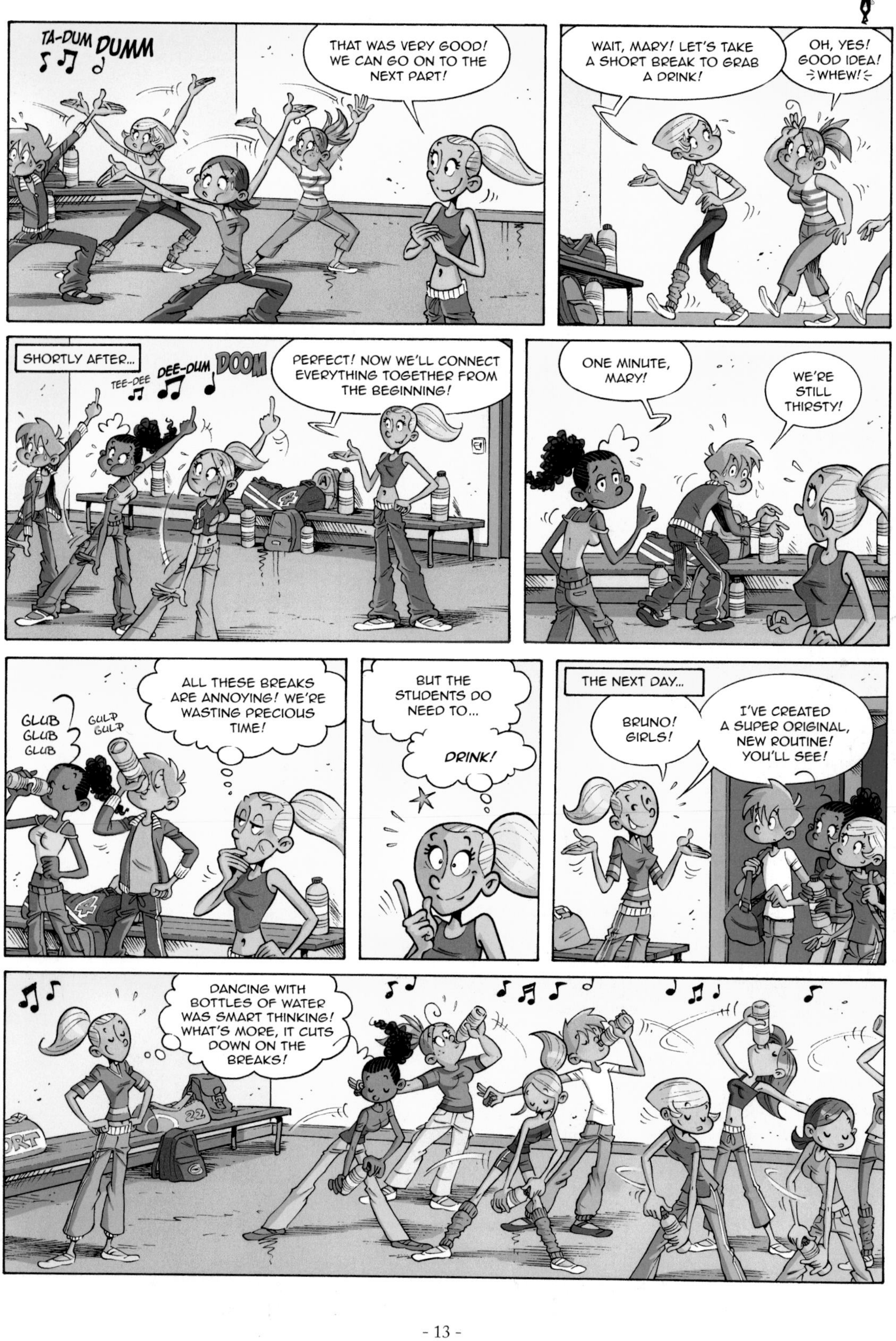
TA-DUM DUMM
THAT WAS VERY GOOD! WE CAN GO ON TO THE NEXT PART!
WAIT, MARY! LET'S TAKE A SHORT BREAK TO GRAB A DRINK!
OH, YES! GOOD IDEA! WHEW!
SHORTLY AFTER...
TEE-DEE DEE-DUM DOOM
PERFECT! NOW WE'LL CONNECT EVERYTHING TOGETHER FROM THE BEGINNING!
ONE MINUTE, MARY!
WE'RE STILL THIRSTY!
GLUB GLUB GLUB
GULP GULP
ALL THESE BREAKS ARE ANNOYING! WE'RE WASTING PRECIOUS TIME!
BUT THE STUDENTS DO NEED TO...
DRINK!
THE NEXT DAY...
BRUNO! GIRLS!
I'VE CREATED A SUPER ORIGINAL, NEW ROUTINE! YOU'LL SEE!
DANCING WITH BOTTLES OF WATER WAS SMART THINKING! WHAT'S MORE, IT CUTS DOWN ON THE BREAKS!

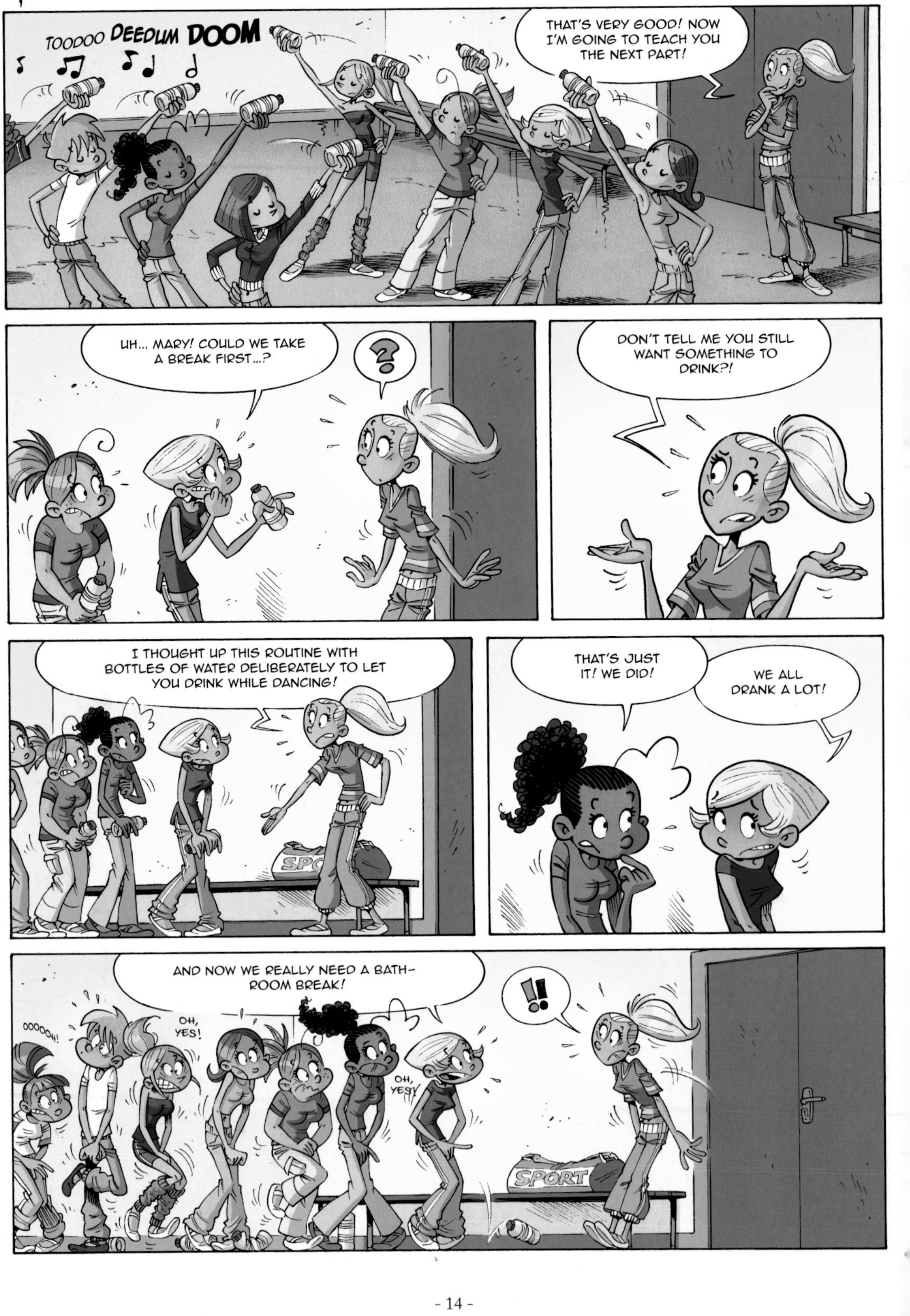
TOODOO DEEDUM DOOM
THAT'S VERY GOOD! NOW I'M GOING TO TEACH YOU THE NEXT PART!
UH... MARY! COULD WE TAKE A BREAK FIRST...?
?
DON'T TELL ME YOU STILL WANT SOMETHING TO DRINK?!
I THOUGHT UP THIS ROUTINE WITH BOTTLES OF WATER DELIBERATELY TO LET YOU DRINK WHILE DANCING!
THAT'S JUST IT! WE DID!
WE ALL DRANK A LOT!
AND NOW WE REALLY NEED A BATH-ROOM BREAK!
!!
OOOOOH!
OH, YES!
OH, YES!
SPORT

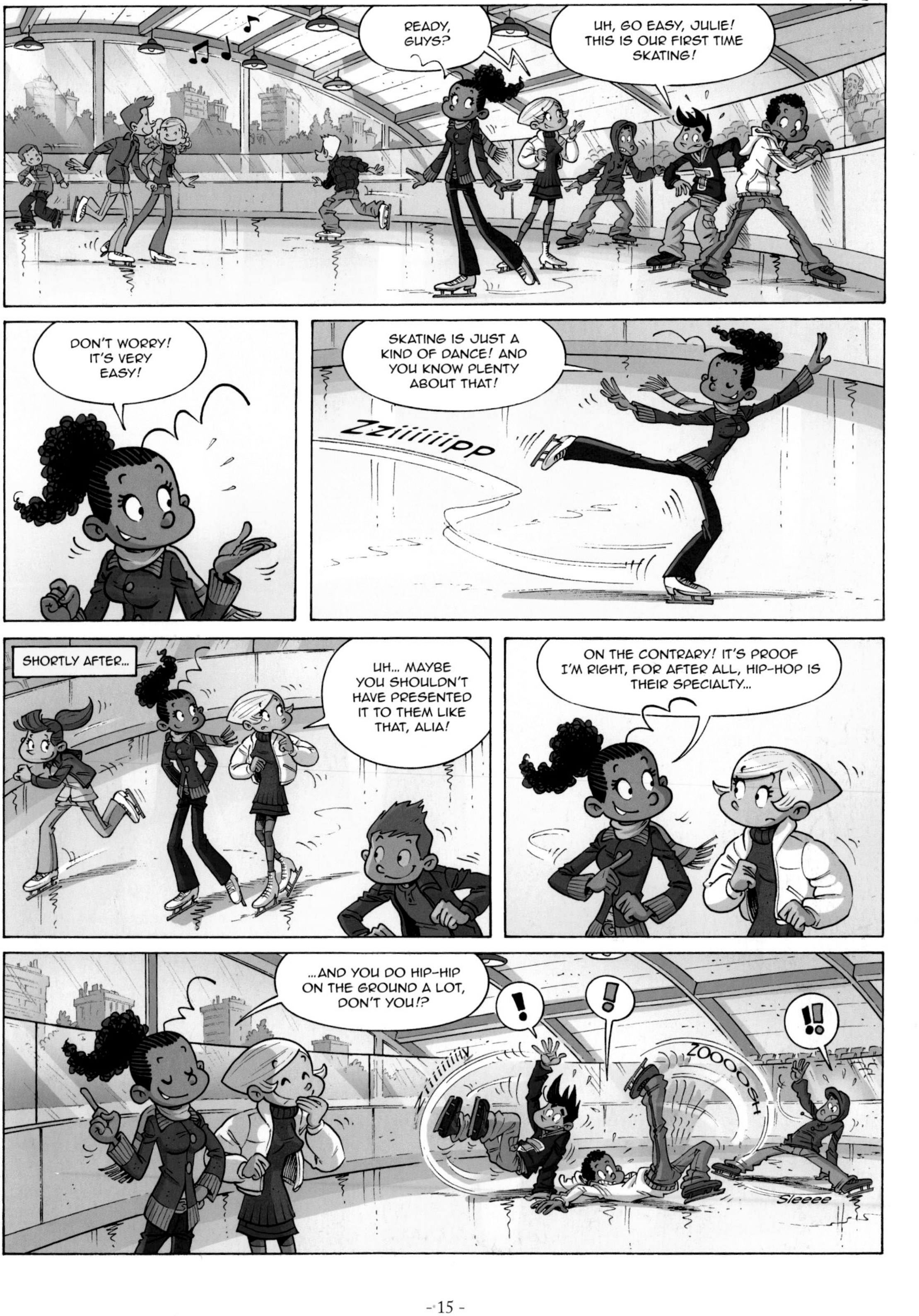
READY, GUYS?
UH, GO EASY, JULIE! THIS IS OUR FIRST TIME SKATING!
DON'T WORRY! IT'S VERY EASY!
SKATING IS JUST A KIND OF DANCE! AND YOU KNOW PLENTY ABOUT THAT!
ZZiiiiiiipp
SHORTLY AFTER...
UH... MAYBE YOU SHOULDN'T HAVE PRESENTED IT TO THEM LIKE THAT, ALIA!
ON THE CONTRARY! IT'S PROOF I'M RIGHT, FOR AFTER ALL, HIP-HOP IS THEIR SPECIALTY...
...AND YOU DO HIP-HIP ON THE GROUND A LOT, DON'T YOU!?
!
!
!!
ZOOOOsh
Sleeee

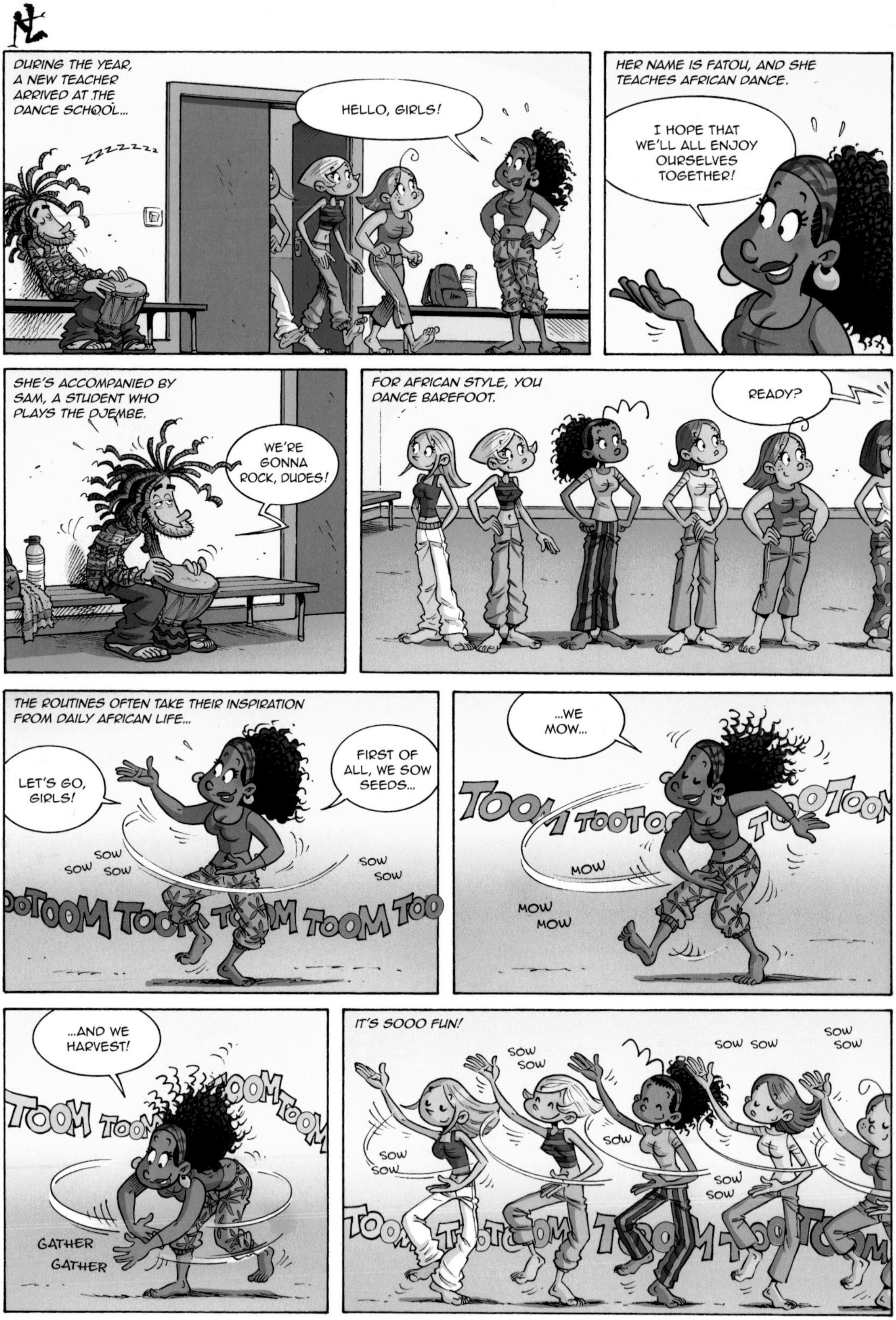
DURING THE YEAR, A NEW TEACHER ARRIVED AT THE DANCE SCHOOL...
ZZZZZZZ
HELLO, GIRLS!
HER NAME IS FATOU, AND SHE TEACHES AFRICAN DANCE.
I HOPE THAT WE'LL ALL ENJOY OURSELVES TOGETHER!
SHE'S ACCOMPANIED BY SAM, A STUDENT WHO PLAYS THE DJEMBE.
WE'RE GONNA ROCK, DUDES!
FOR AFRICAN STYLE, YOU DANCE BAREFOOT.
READY?
THE ROUTINES OFTEN TAKE THEIR INSPIRATION FROM DAILY AFRICAN LIFE...
LET'S GO, GIRLS!
FIRST OF ALL, WE SOW SEEDS...
SOW SOW SOW
SOW SOW
TOOTOOM TOOM TOOM TOOM TOO
...WE MOW...
TOOM TOOTOO TOOTOOM
MOW
MOW MOW
...AND WE HARVEST!
TOOM TOOM TOOMTOOM
GATHER GATHER
IT'S SOOO FUN!
SOW SOW
SOW SOW
SOW SOW
SOW
SOW SOW
SOW SOW
TOOM TOOTOOM TOOM TOOTOOM

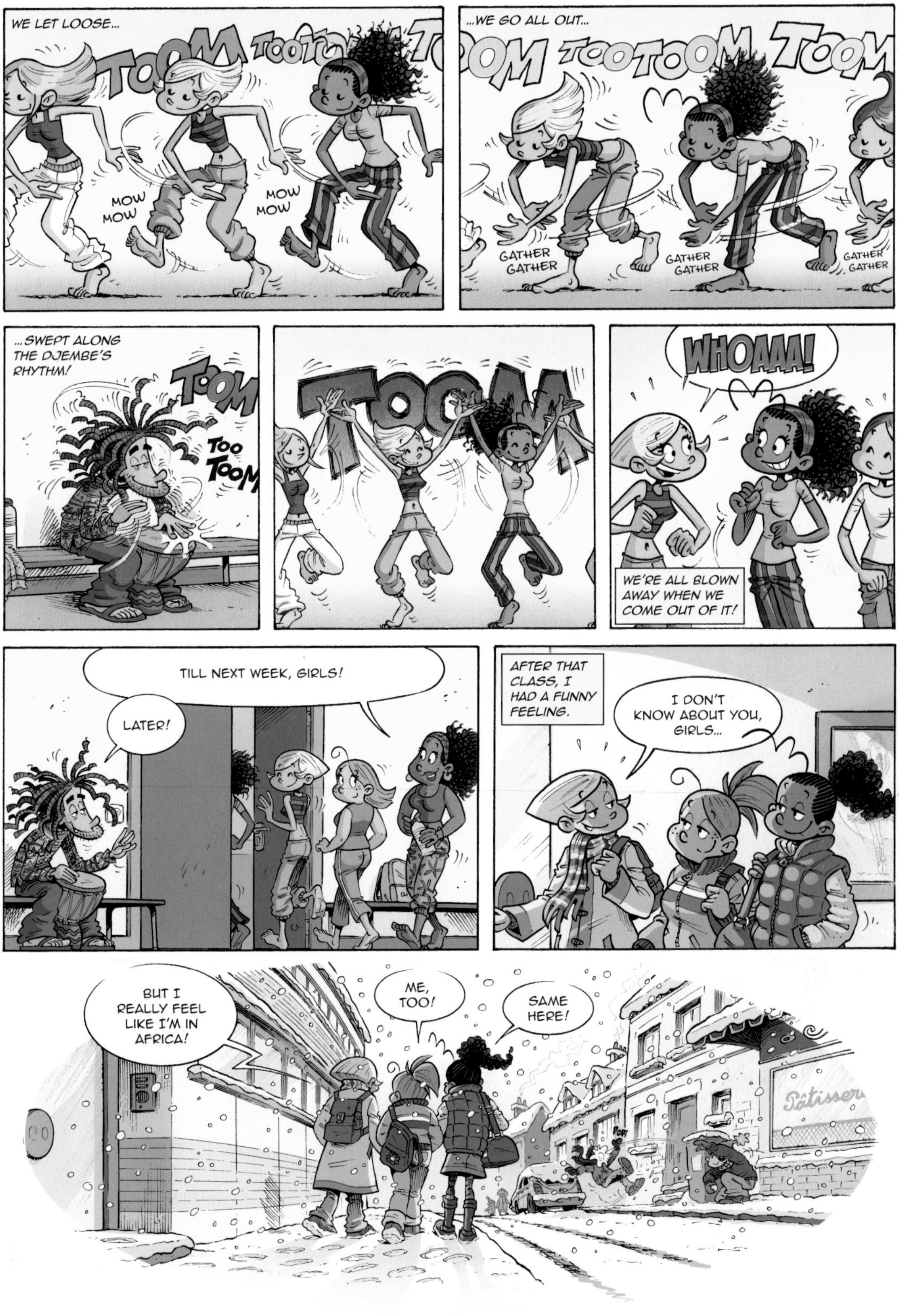
WE LET LOOSE...
TOOM TOOTOOM TOOM
MOW MOW
MOW MOW
...WE GO ALL OUT...
TOOM TOOTOOM TOOM
GATHER GATHER
GATHER GATHER
GATHER GATHER
...SWEPT ALONG THE DJEMBE'S RHYTHM!
TOOM
TOO TOOM
TOOM
WHOAAA!
WE'RE ALL BLOWN AWAY WHEN WE COME OUT OF IT!
TILL NEXT WEEK, GIRLS!
LATER!
AFTER THAT CLASS, I HAD A FUNNY FEELING.
I DON'T KNOW ABOUT YOU, GIRLS...
BUT I REALLY FEEL LIKE I'M IN AFRICA!
ME, TOO!
SAME HERE!

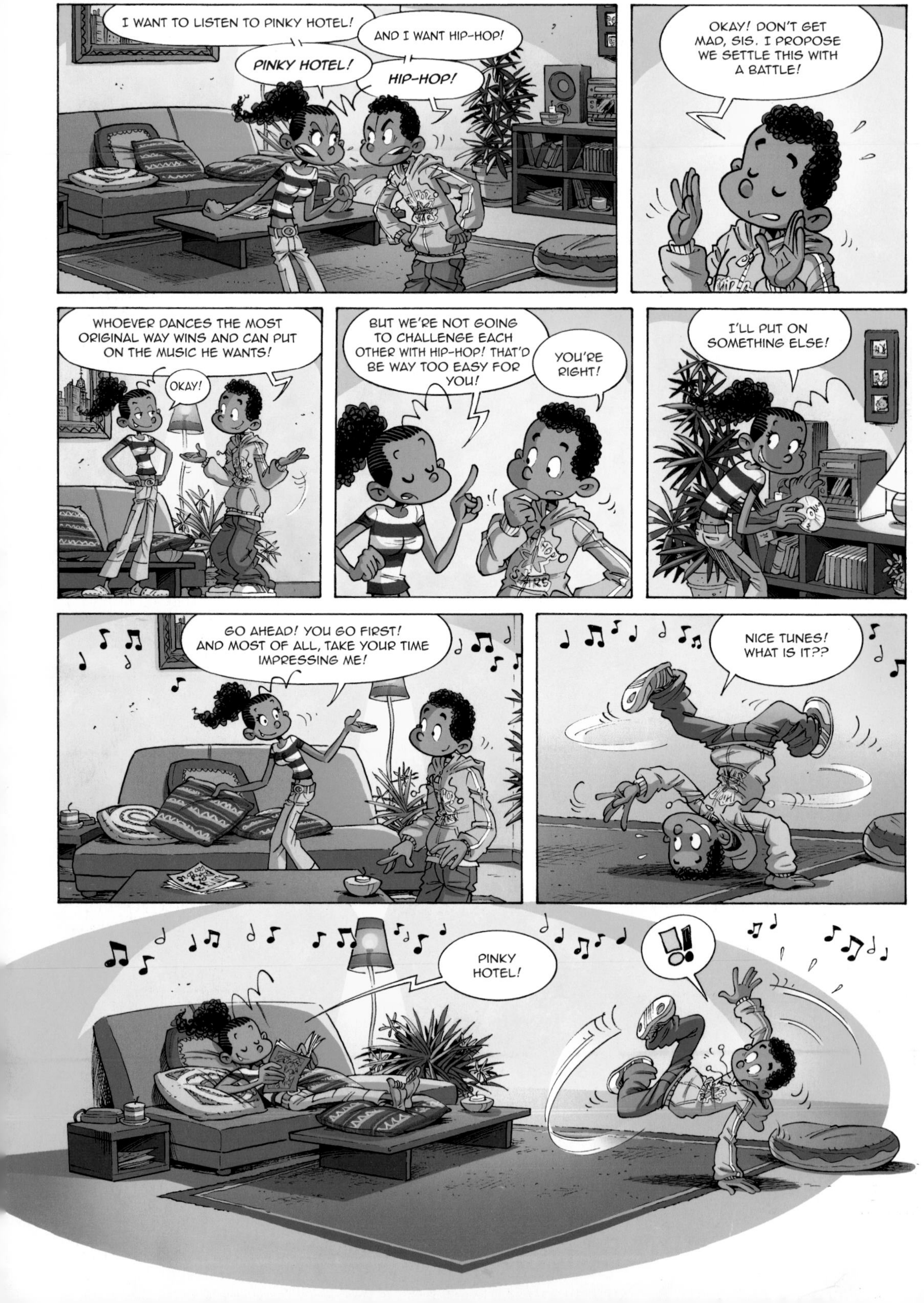
I WANT TO LISTEN TO PINKY HOTEL!
AND I WANT HIP-HOP!
PINKY HOTEL!
HIP-HOP!
OKAY! DON'T GET MAD, SIS. I PROPOSE WE SETTLE THIS WITH A BATTLE!
WHOEVER DANCES THE MOST ORIGINAL WAY WINS AND CAN PUT ON THE MUSIC HE WANTS!
OKAY!
BUT WE'RE NOT GOING TO CHALLENGE EACH OTHER WITH HIP-HOP! THAT'D BE WAY TOO EASY FOR YOU!
YOU'RE RIGHT!
I'LL PUT ON SOMETHING ELSE!
GO AHEAD! YOU GO FIRST! AND MOST OF ALL, TAKE YOUR TIME IMPRESSING ME!
NICE TUNES! WHAT IS IT??
PINKY HOTEL!
!!

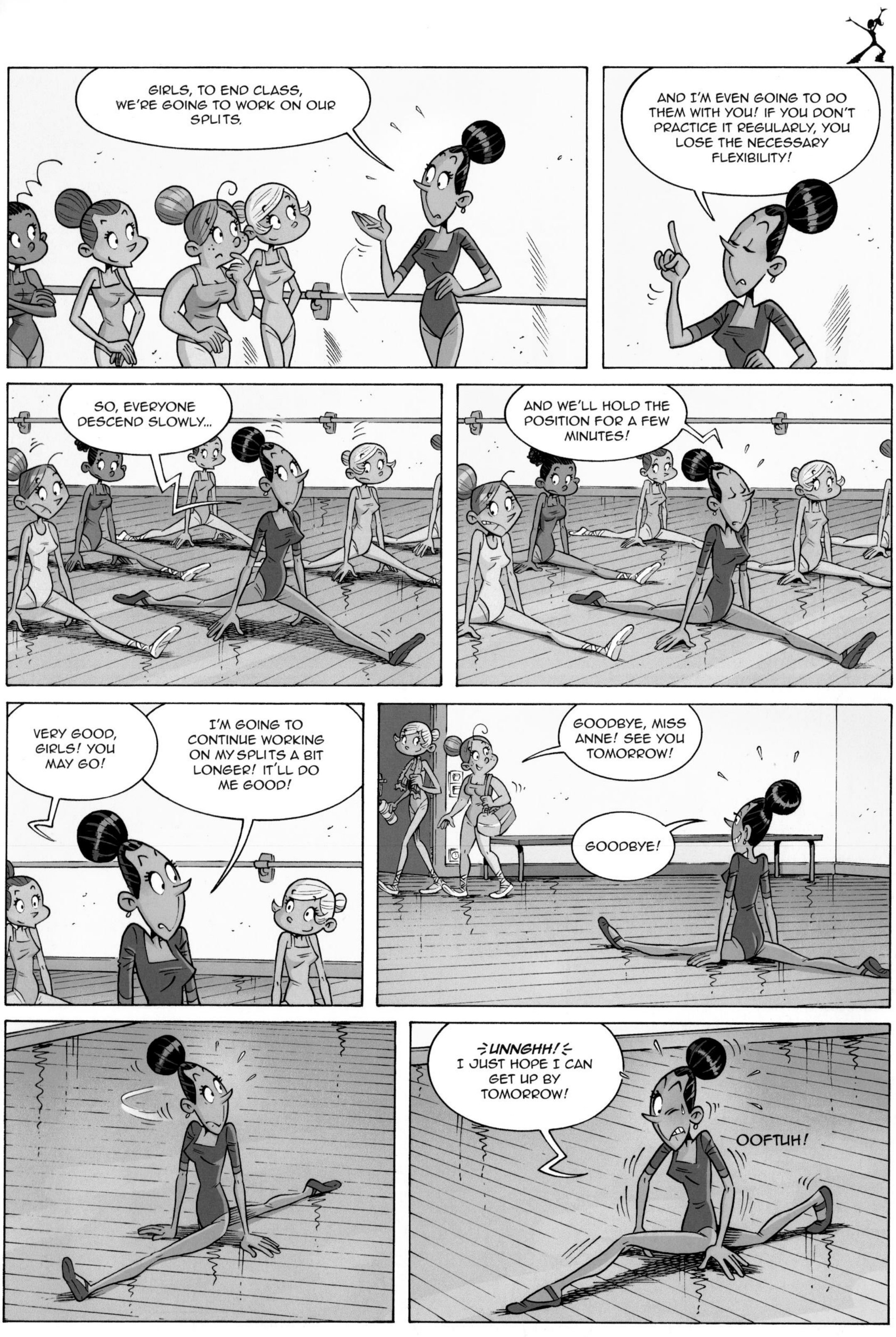
GIRLS, TO END CLASS, WE'RE GOING TO WORK ON OUR SPLITS.
AND I'M EVEN GOING TO DO THEM WITH YOU! IF YOU DON'T PRACTICE IT REGULARLY, YOU LOSE THE NECESSARY FLEXIBILITY!
SO, EVERYONE DESCEND SLOWLY...
AND WE'LL HOLD THE POSITION FOR A FEW MINUTES!
VERY GOOD, GIRLS! YOU MAY GO!
I'M GOING TO CONTINUE WORKING ON MY SPLITS A BIT LONGER! IT'LL DO ME GOOD!
GOODBYE, MISS ANNE! SEE YOU TOMORROW!
GOODBYE!
UNNGHH!
I JUST HOPE I CAN GET UP BY TOMORROW!
OOFTUH!

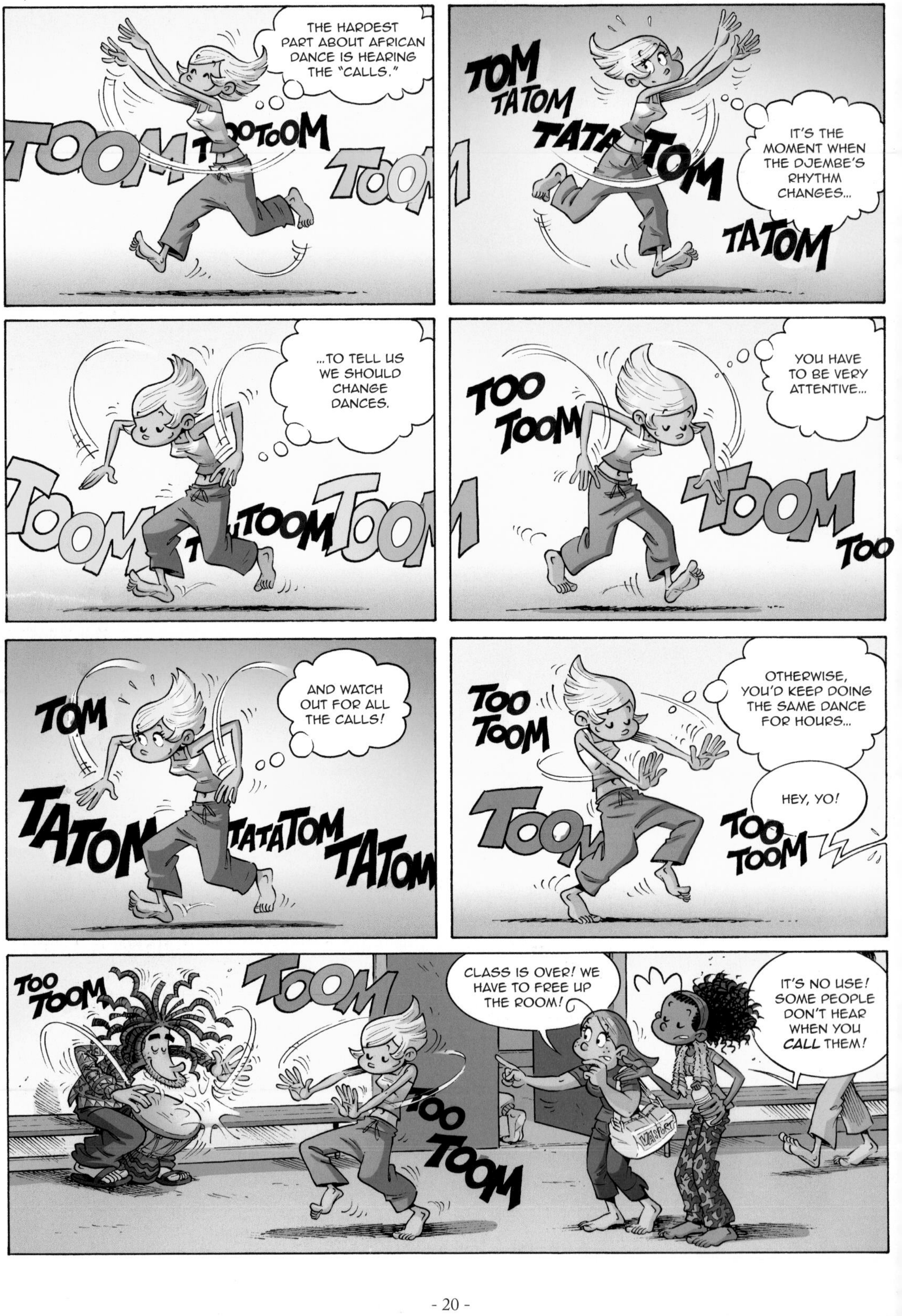
THE HARDEST PART ABOUT AFRICAN DANCE IS HEARING THE "CALLS."
TOOM
TOOM
TOM
TATOM
IT'S THE MOMENT WHEN THE DJEMBE'S RHYTHM CHANGES...
TOM
TATOM
...TO TELL US WE SHOULD CHANGE DANCES.
TOOM
TOOM
TOO
TOOM
YOU HAVE TO BE VERY ATTENTIVE...
TOOM
TOO
TOM
AND WATCH OUT FOR ALL THE CALLS!
TATATOM
TATOM
TOO
TOOM
OTHERWISE, YOU'D KEEP DOING THE SAME DANCE FOR HOURS...
HEY, YO!
TOO
TOOM
TOO
TOOM
TOOM
CLASS IS OVER! WE HAVE TO FREE UP THE ROOM!
IT'S NO USE! SOME PEOPLE DON'T HEAR WHEN YOU CALL THEM!
TOO
TOOM

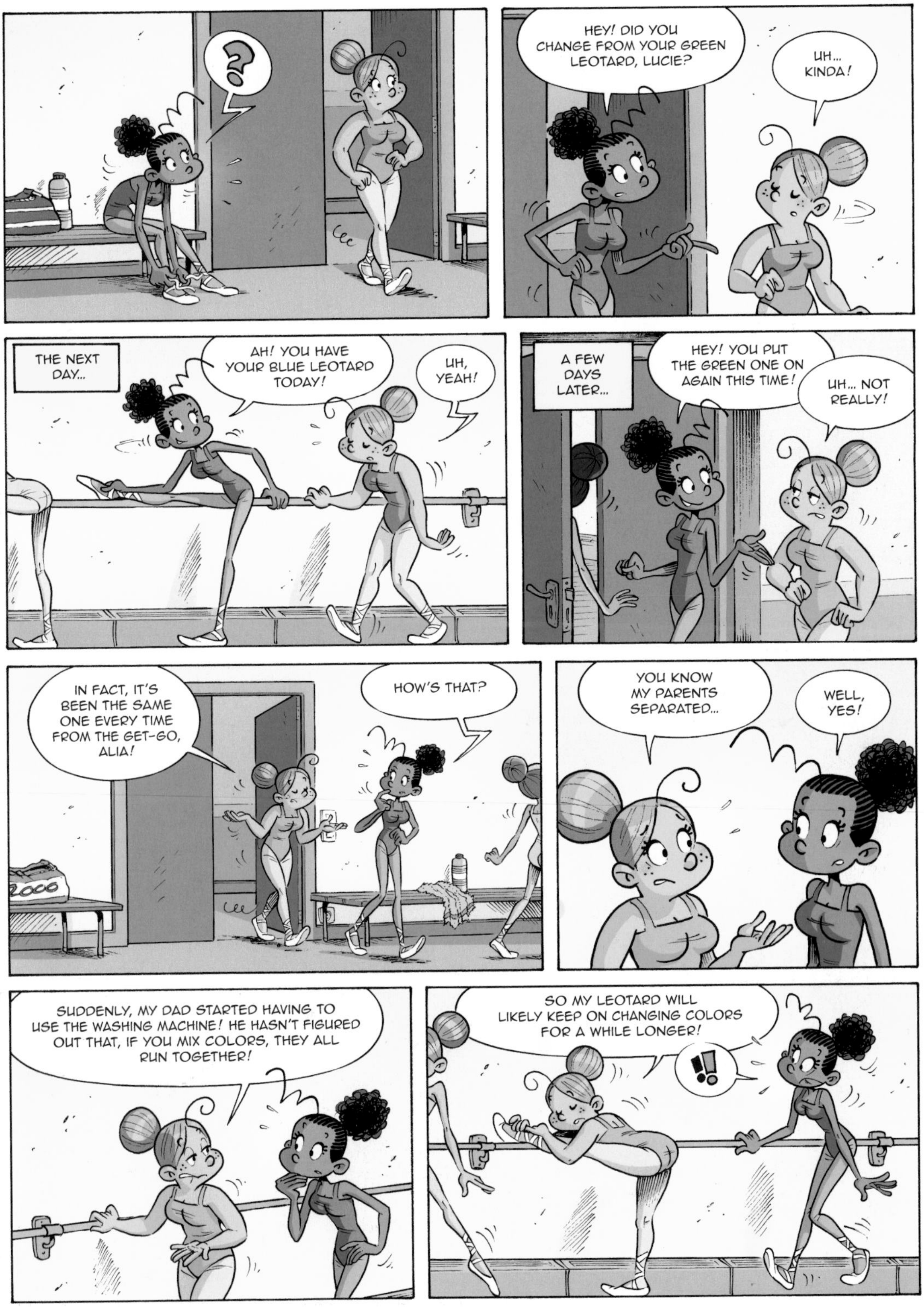
?
HEY! DID YOU CHANGE FROM YOUR GREEN LEOTARD, LUCIE?
UH... KINDA!
THE NEXT DAY...
AH! YOU HAVE YOUR BLUE LEOTARD TODAY!
UH, YEAH!
A FEW DAYS LATER...
HEY! YOU PUT THE GREEN ONE ON AGAIN THIS TIME!
UH... NOT REALLY!
IN FACT, IT'S BEEN THE SAME ONE EVERY TIME FROM THE GET-GO, ALIA!
HOW'S THAT?
YOU KNOW MY PARENTS SEPARATED...
WELL, YES!
SUDDENLY, MY DAD STARTED HAVING TO USE THE WASHING MACHINE! HE HASN'T FIGURED OUT THAT, IF YOU MIX COLORS, THEY ALL RUN TOGETHER!
SO MY LEOTARD WILL LIKELY KEEP ON CHANGING COLORS FOR A WHILE LONGER!
!!

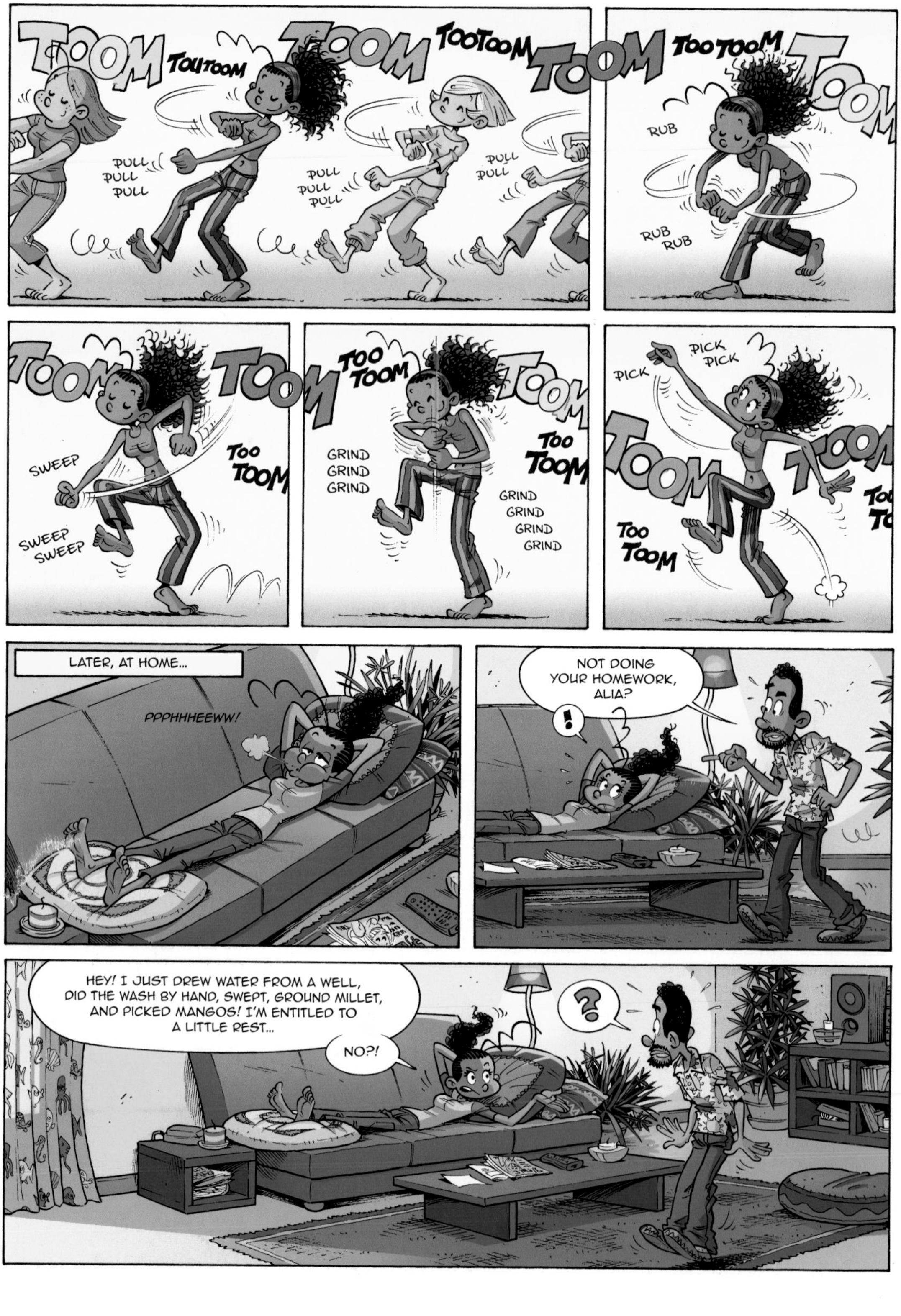
TOOM
TOUTOOM
PULL PULL PULL
TOOM
PULL PULL PULL
TOOTOOM
PULL PULL
TOOM
TOOTOOM
TOOM
RUB
RUB RUB
TOOM
SWEEP
SWEEP SWEEP
TOOM
TOO TOOM
TOO TOOM
GRIND GRIND GRIND
TOOM
TOO TOOM
GRIND GRIND GRIND GRIND
PICK
PICK PICK
TOOM
TOO TOOM
TOOM
LATER, AT HOME...
PPPHHHEEWW!
NOT DOING YOUR HOMEWORK, ALIA?
!
HEY! I JUST DREW WATER FROM A WELL, DID THE WASH BY HAND, SWEPT, GROUND MILLET, AND PICKED MANGOS! I'M ENTITLED TO A LITTLE REST...
NO?!
?

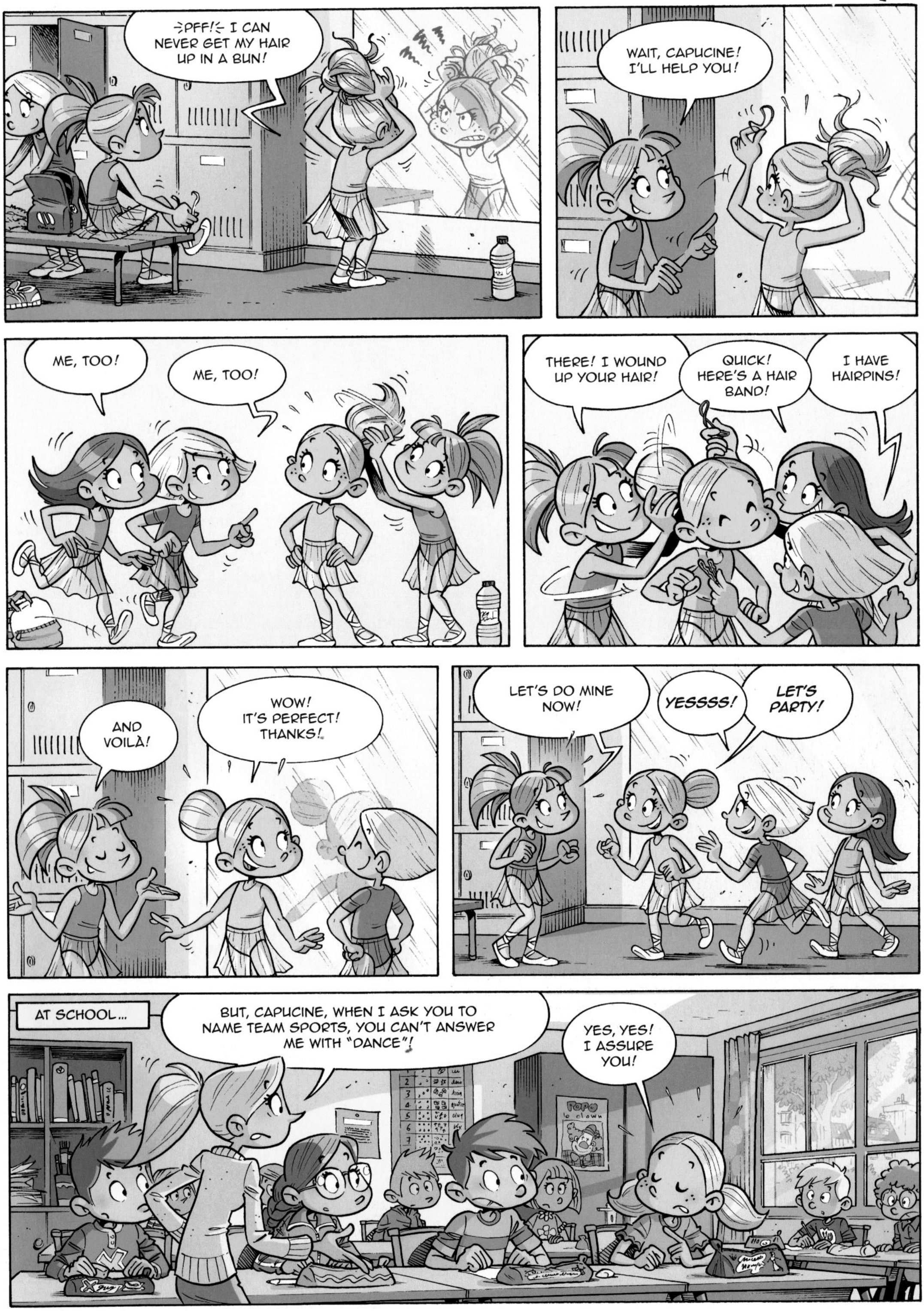
PFF! I CAN NEVER GET MY HAIR UP IN A BUN!
WAIT, CAPUCINE! I'LL HELP YOU!
ME, TOO!
ME, TOO!
THERE! I WOUND UP YOUR HAIR!
QUICK! HERE'S A HAIR BAND!
I HAVE HAIRPINS!
AND VOILÀ!
WOW! IT'S PERFECT! THANKS!
LET'S DO MINE NOW!
YESSSS!
LET'S PARTY!
AT SCHOOL...
BUT, CAPUCINE, WHEN I ASK YOU TO NAME TEAM SPORTS, YOU CAN'T ANSWER ME WITH "DANCE"!
YES, YES! I ASSURE YOU!

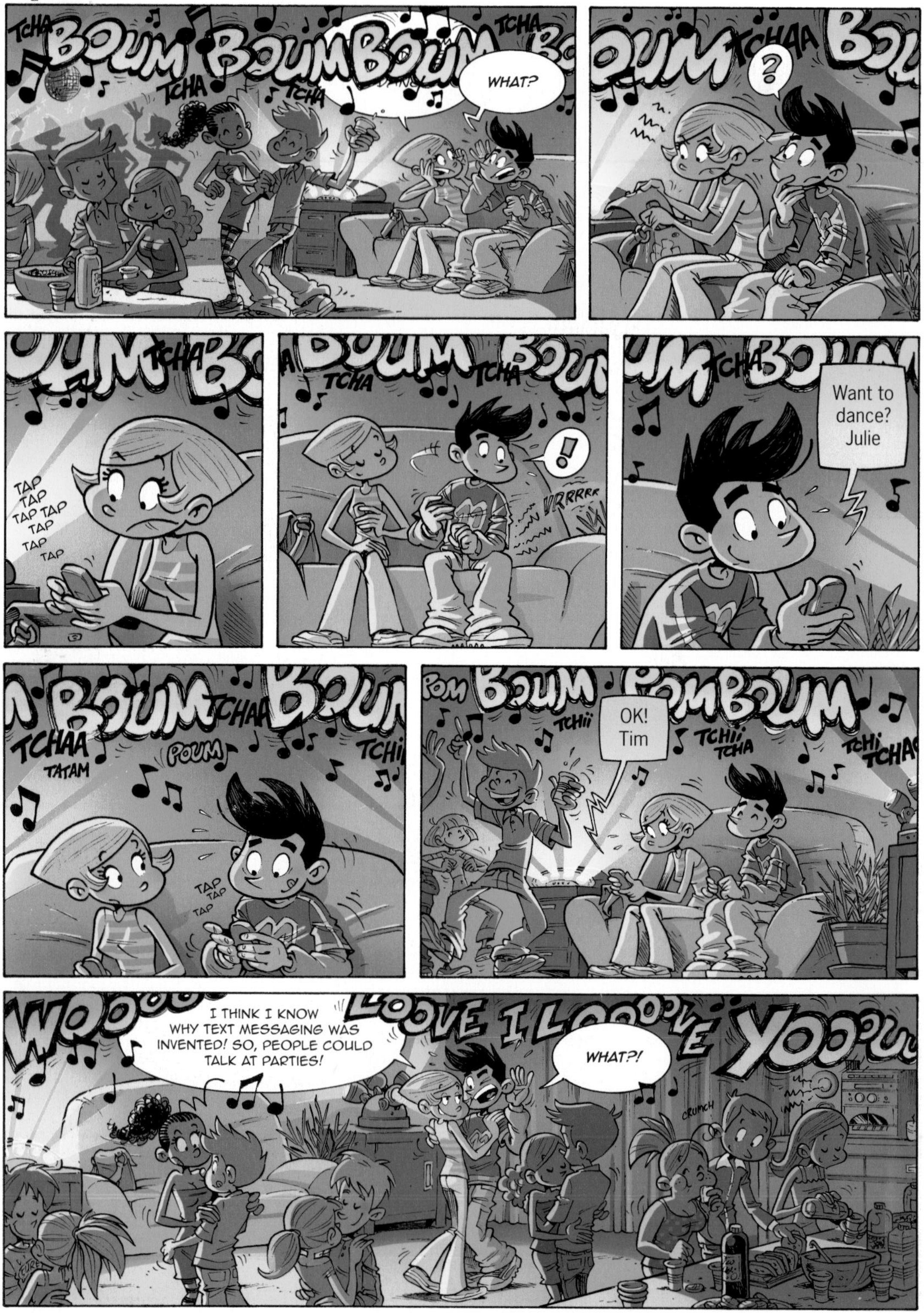
TCHA
BOUM BOUMBOUM
TCHA
TCHA
TCHA
WHAT?
OUM
TCHAA
BOU
?
OUM
TCHA
BO
TAP TAP TAP TAP TAP TAP TAP
BOUM
TCHA
TCHA
BOU
!
VRRRRR
UM
TCHA
BOUM
Want to dance? Julie
BOUM
TCHAA
BOUM
TCHAA
TATAM
POUM
TCHI
TAP TAP TAP
POM BOUM
POMBOUM
TCHII
OK! Tim
TCHII TCHA
TCHI TCHA
WOOO
LOOOVE I LOOOVE YOOOU
I THINK I KNOW WHY TEXT MESSAGING WAS INVENTED! SO, PEOPLE COULD TALK AT PARTIES!
WHAT?!
CRUMCH

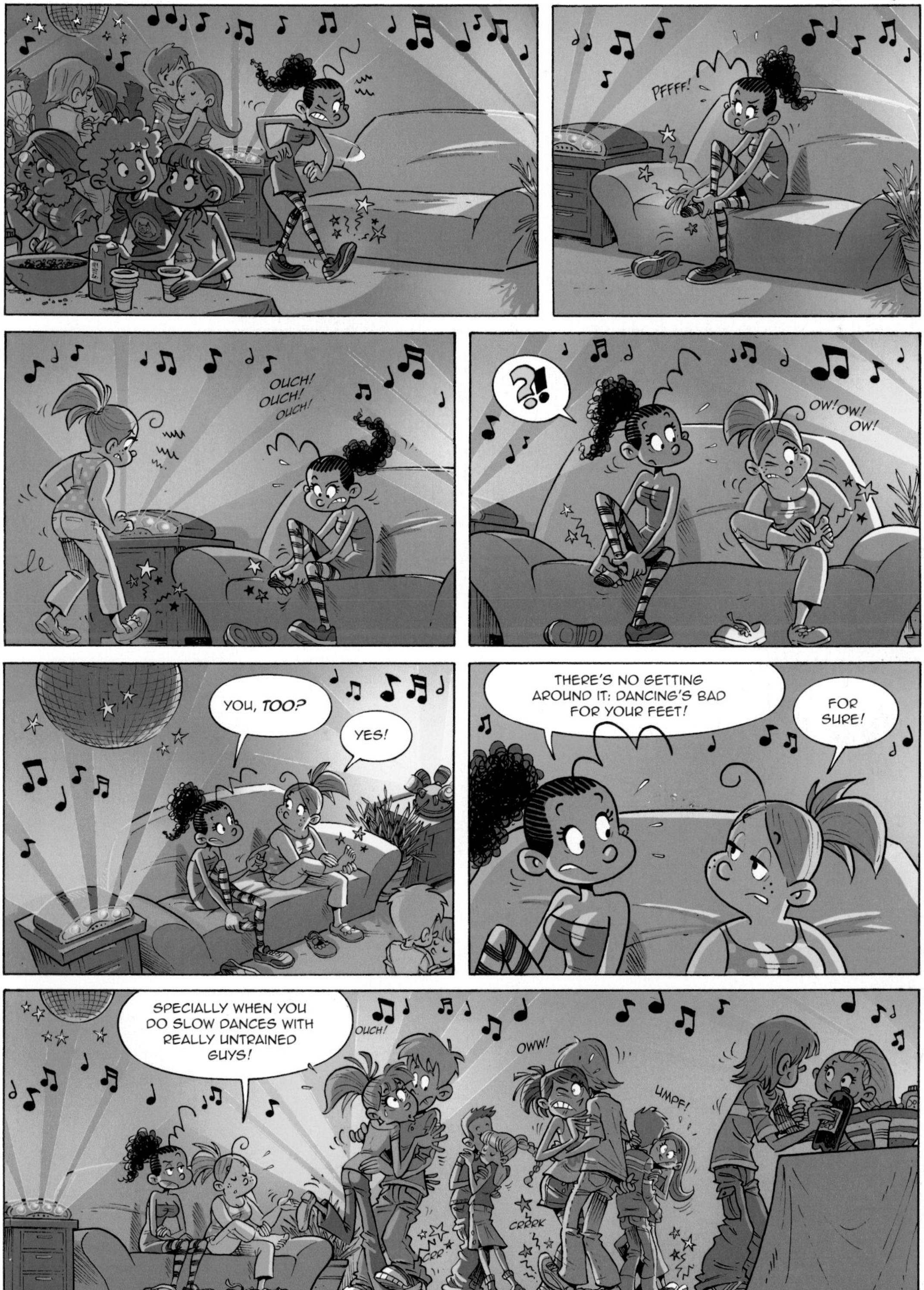
PFFFF!
OUCH! OUCH! OUCH!
?!
OW! OW! OW!
YOU, TOO?
YES!
THERE'S NO GETTING AROUND IT: DANCING'S BAD FOR YOUR FEET!
FOR SURE!
SPECIALLY WHEN YOU DO SLOW DANCES WITH REALLY UNTRAINED GUYS!
OUCH!
OWW!
UMPF!
CRR
CRRRK

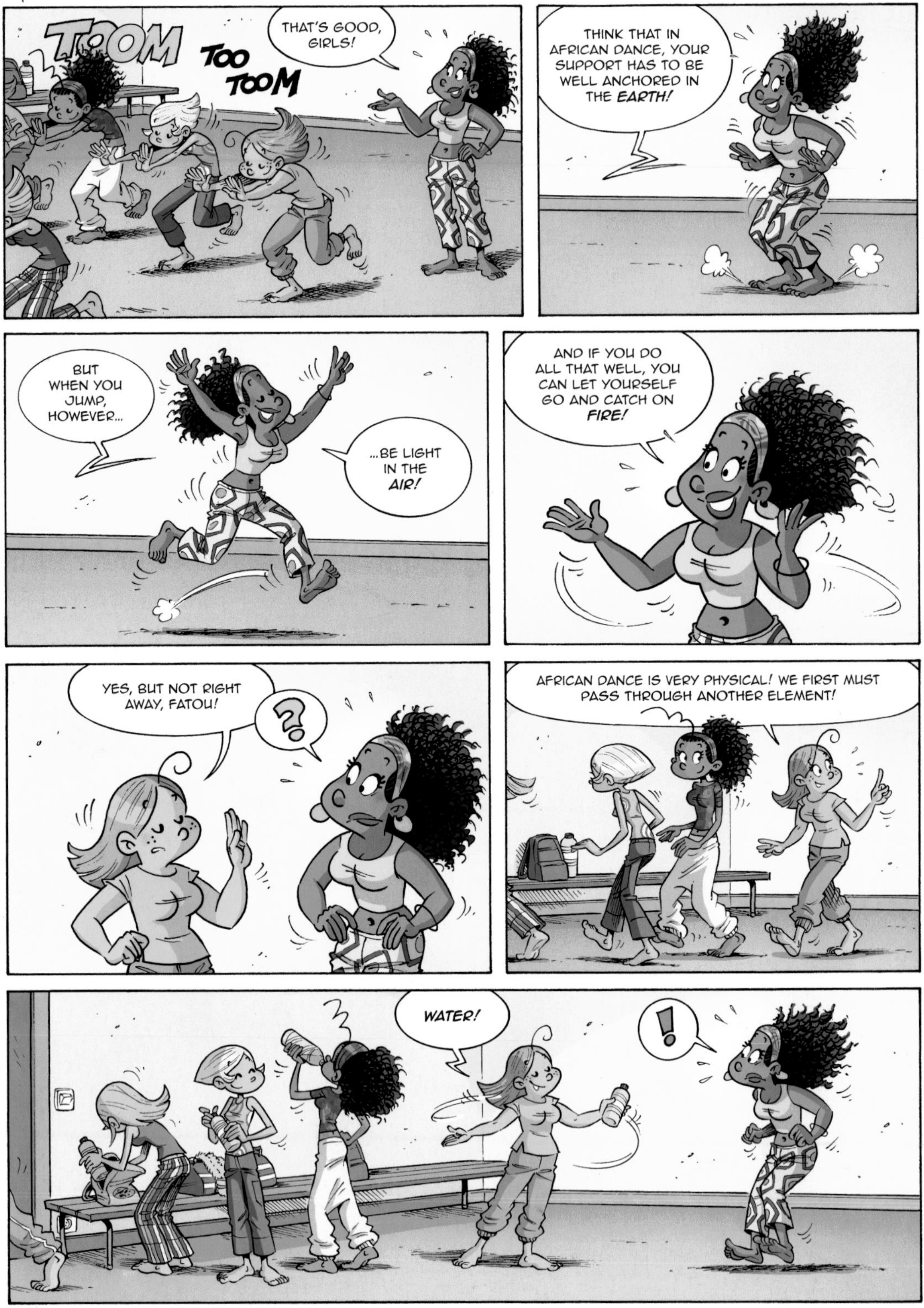
TOOM
TOO TOOM
THAT'S GOOD, GIRLS!
THINK THAT IN AFRICAN DANCE, YOUR SUPPORT HAS TO BE WELL ANCHORED IN THE EARTH!
BUT WHEN YOU JUMP, HOWEVER...
...BE LIGHT IN THE AIR!
AND IF YOU DO ALL THAT WELL, YOU CAN LET YOURSELF GO AND CATCH ON FIRE!
YES, BUT NOT RIGHT AWAY, FATOU!
?
AFRICAN DANCE IS VERY PHYSICAL! WE FIRST MUST PASS THROUGH ANOTHER ELEMENT!
WATER!
!

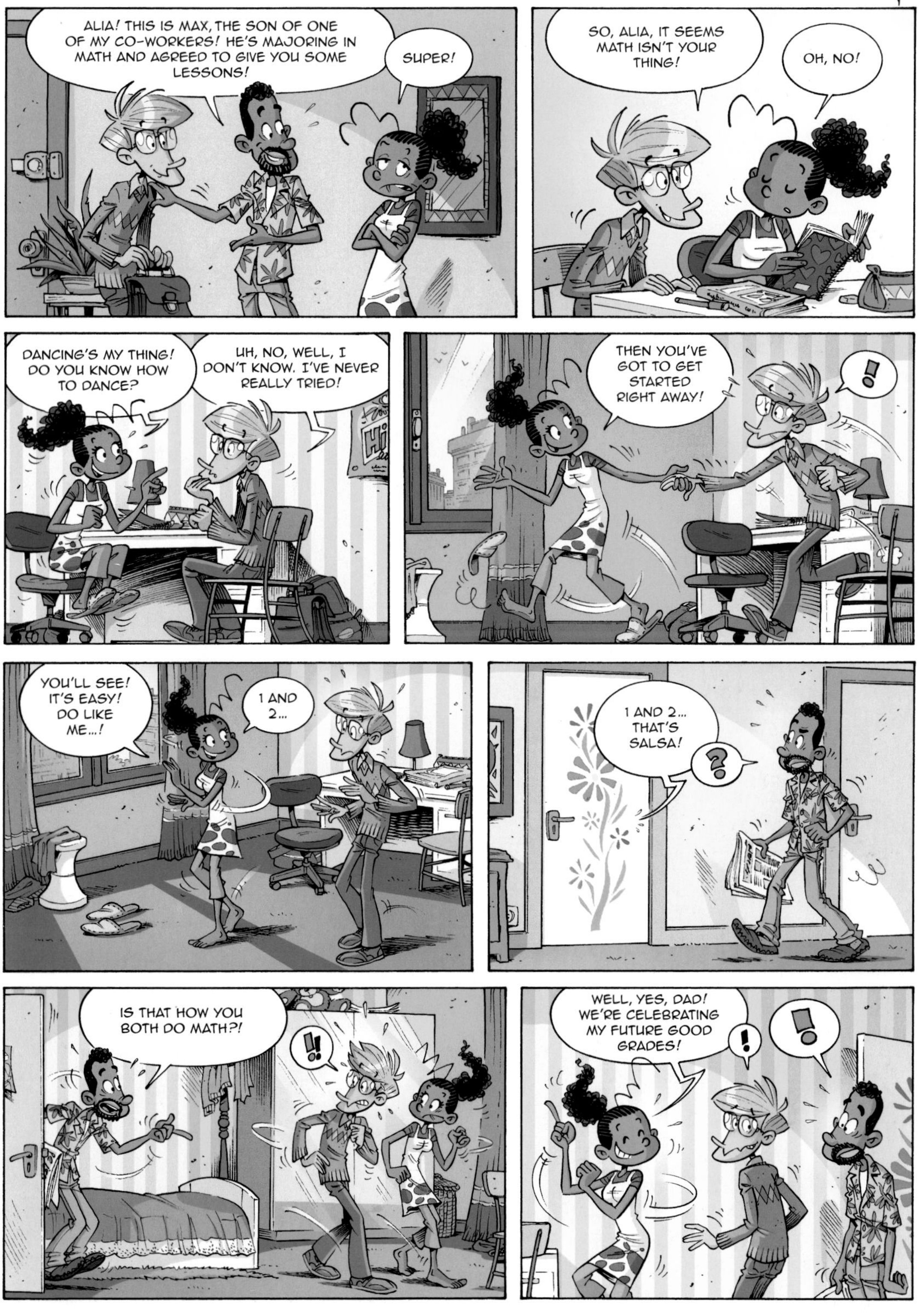
ALIA! THIS IS MAX, THE SON OF ONE OF MY CO-WORKERS! HE'S MAJORING IN MATH AND AGREED TO GIVE YOU SOME LESSONS!
SUPER!
SO, ALIA, IT SEEMS MATH ISN'T YOUR THING!
OH, NO!
DANCING'S MY THING! DO YOU KNOW HOW TO DANCE?
UH, NO, WELL, I DON'T KNOW. I'VE NEVER REALLY TRIED!
THEN YOU'VE GOT TO GET STARTED RIGHT AWAY!
!
YOU'LL SEE! IT'S EASY! DO LIKE ME...!
1 AND 2...
1 AND 2... THAT'S SALSA!
?
IS THAT HOW YOU BOTH DO MATH?!
!!
WELL, YES, DAD! WE'RE CELEBRATING MY FUTURE GOOD GRADES!
!
!

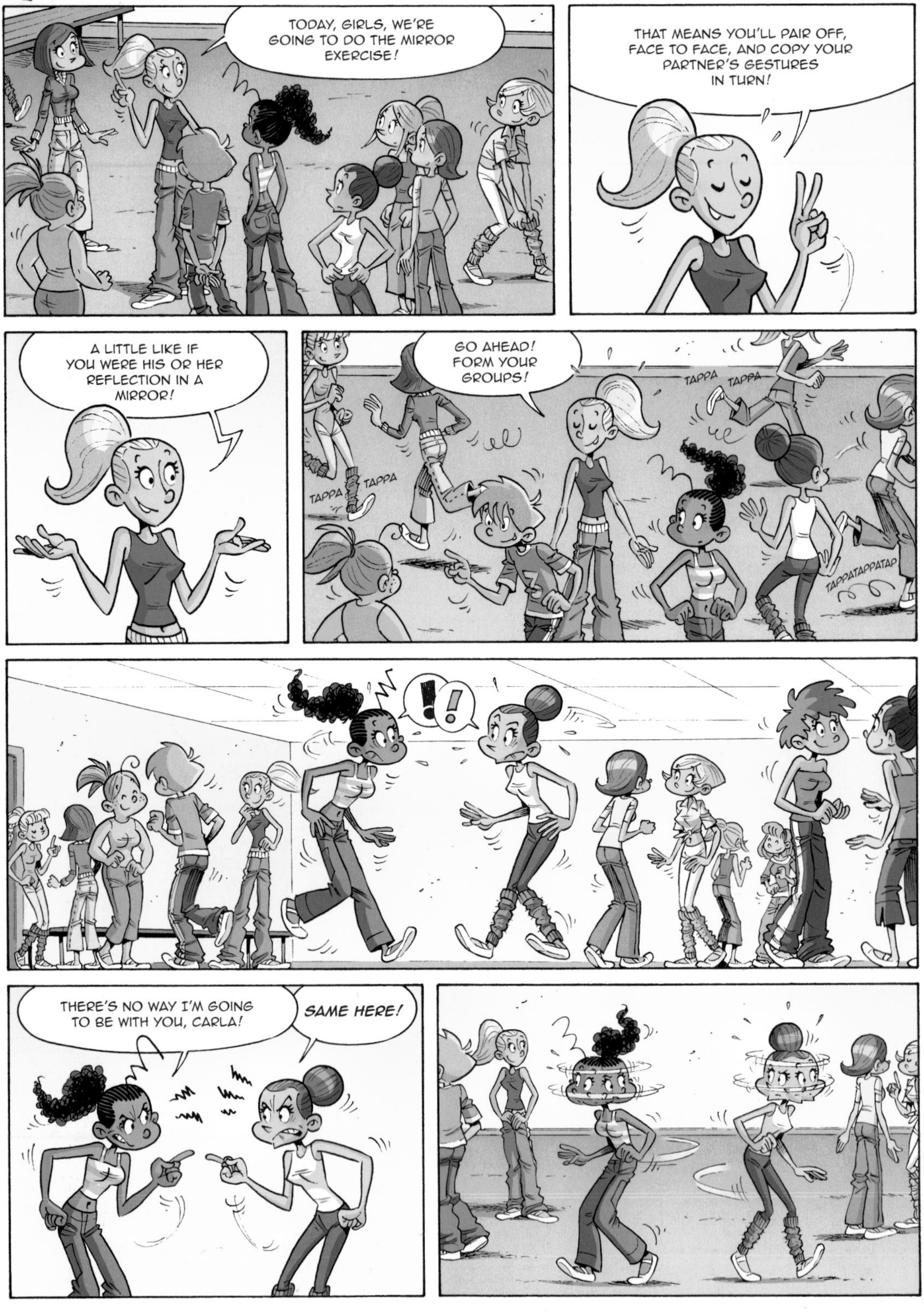
TODAY, GIRLS, WE'RE GOING TO DO THE MIRROR EXERCISE!
THAT MEANS YOU'LL PAIR OFF, FACE TO FACE, AND COPY YOUR PARTNER'S GESTURES IN TURN!
A LITTLE LIKE IF YOU WERE HIS OR HER REFLECTION IN A MIRROR!
GO AHEAD! FORM YOUR GROUPS!
TAPPA TAPPA
TAPPA TAPPA
TAPPATAPPATAP
!
!
THERE'S NO WAY I'M GOING TO BE WITH YOU, CARLA!
SAME HERE!

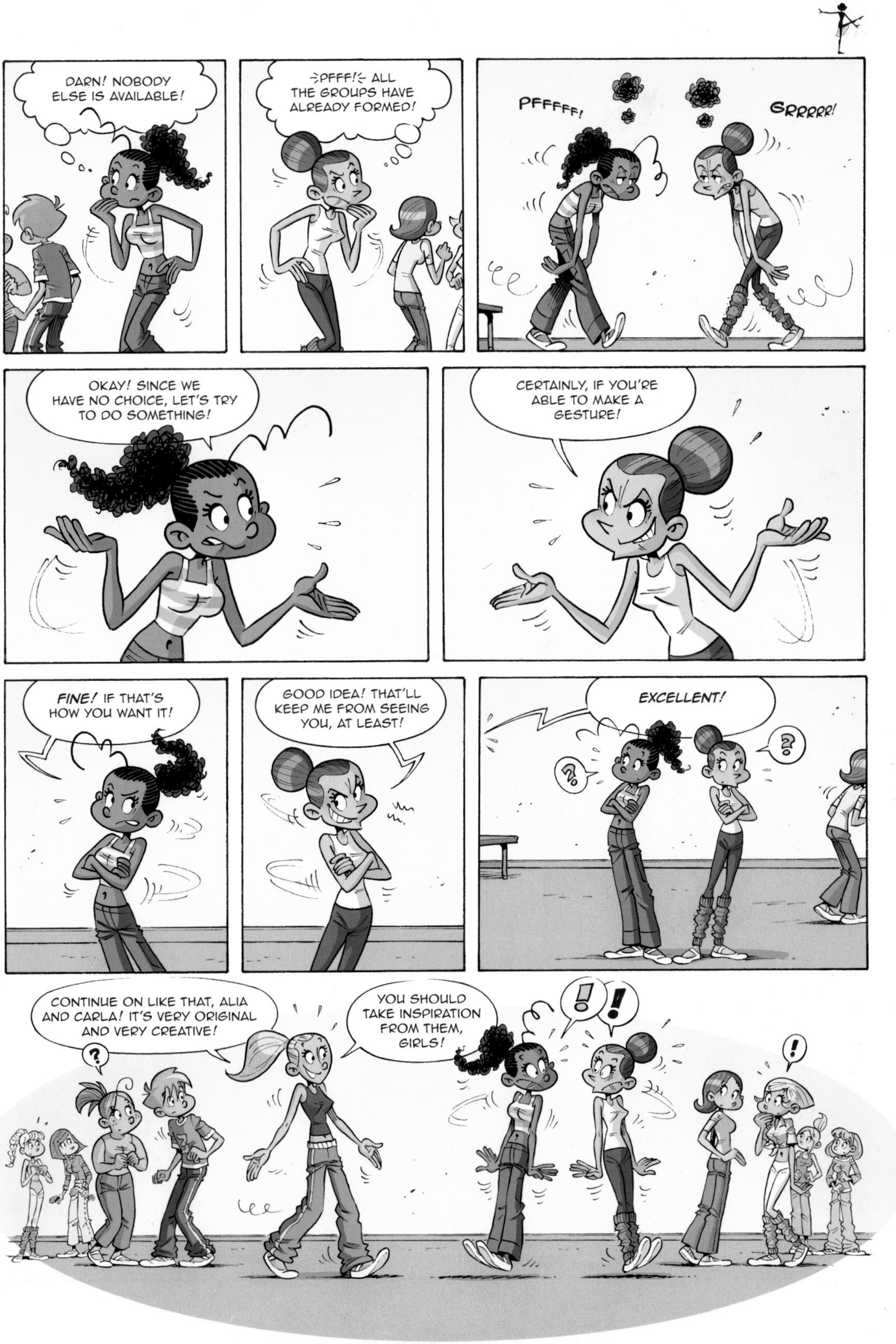
DARN! NOBODY ELSE IS AVAILABLE!
PFFF! ALL THE GROUPS HAVE ALREADY FORMED!
PFFFFF!
GRRRRR!
OKAY! SINCE WE HAVE NO CHOICE, LET'S TRY TO DO SOMETHING!
CERTAINLY, IF YOU'RE ABLE TO MAKE A GESTURE!
FINE! IF THAT'S HOW YOU WANT IT!
GOOD IDEA! THAT'LL KEEP ME FROM SEEING YOU, AT LEAST!
EXCELLENT!
?
?
CONTINUE ON LIKE THAT, ALIA AND CARLA! IT'S VERY ORIGINAL AND VERY CREATIVE!
?
YOU SHOULD TAKE INSPIRATION FROM THEM, GIRLS!
!
!
!

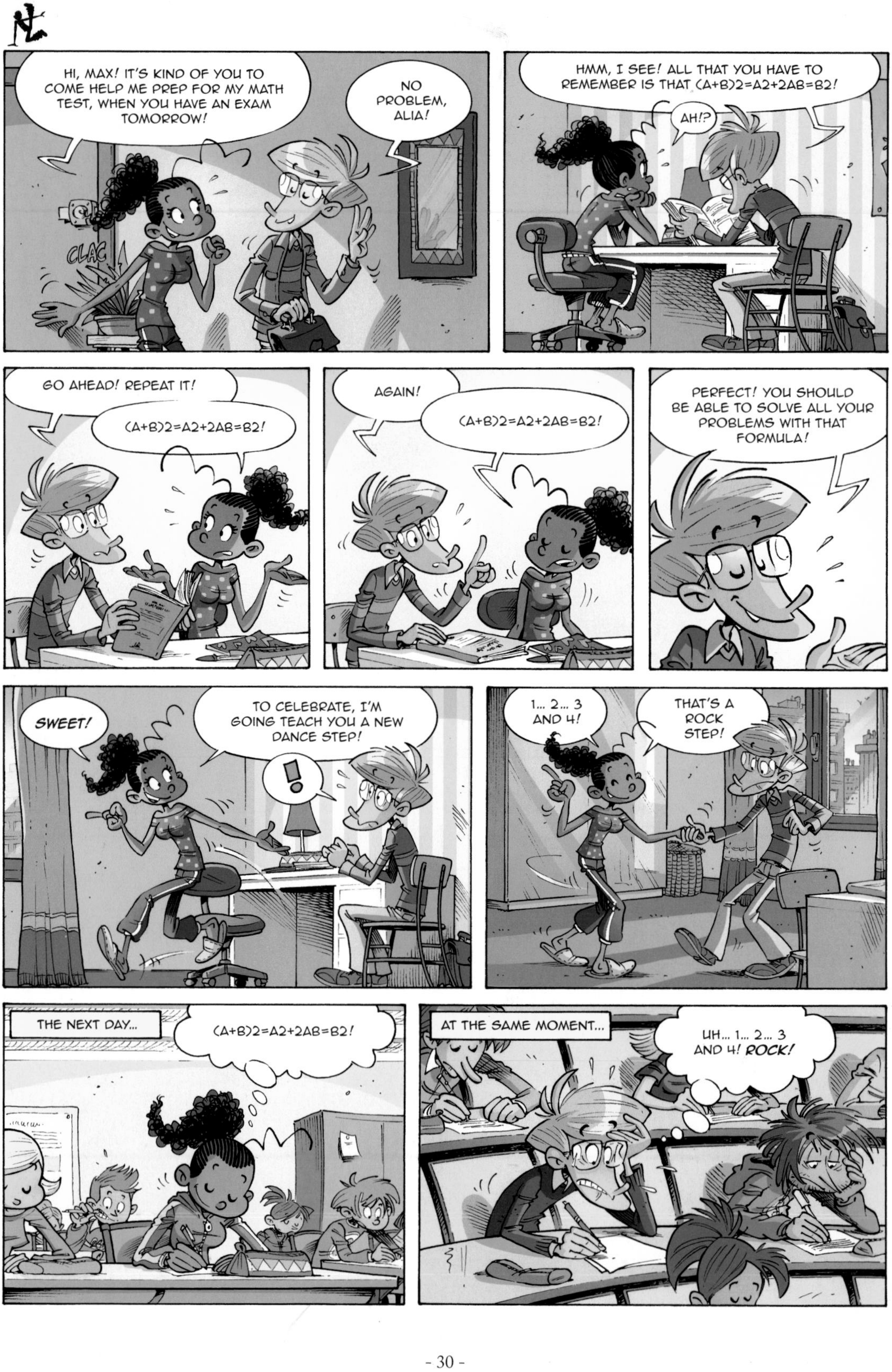
HI, MAX! IT'S KIND OF YOU TO COME HELP ME PREP FOR MY MATH TEST, WHEN YOU HAVE AN EXAM TOMORROW!
NO PROBLEM, ALIA!
CLAC
HMM, I SEE! ALL THAT YOU HAVE TO REMEMBER IS THAT (A+B)2=A2+2AB=B2!
AH!?
GO AHEAD! REPEAT IT!
(A+B)2=A2+2AB=B2!
AGAIN!
(A+B)2=A2+2AB=B2!
PERFECT! YOU SHOULD BE ABLE TO SOLVE ALL YOUR PROBLEMS WITH THAT FORMULA!
SWEET!
TO CELEBRATE, I'M GOING TEACH YOU A NEW DANCE STEP!
!
1... 2... 3 AND 4!
THAT'S A ROCK STEP!
THE NEXT DAY...
(A+B)2=A2+2AB=B2!
AT THE SAME MOMENT...
UH... 1... 2... 3 AND 4! ROCK!

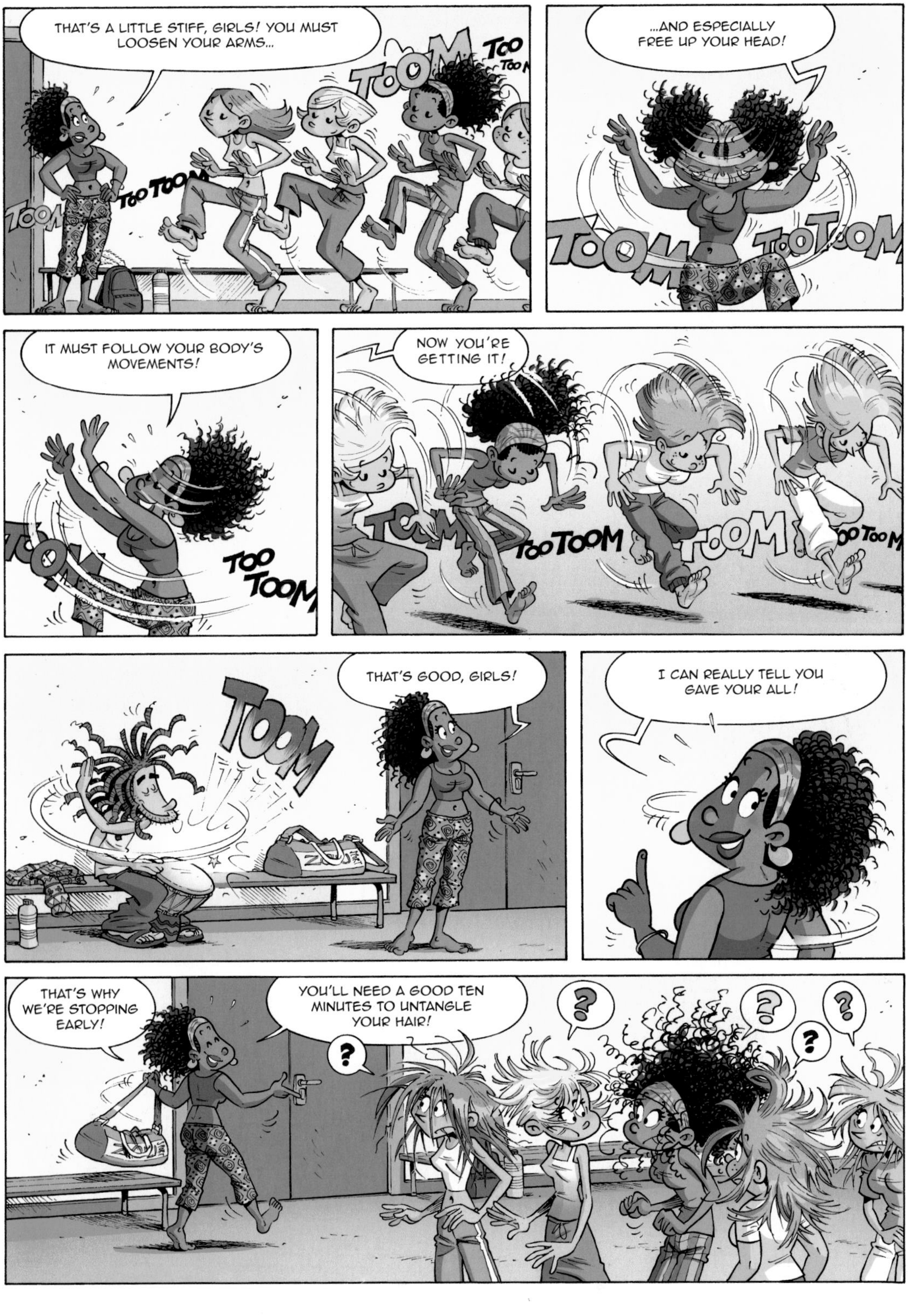
THAT'S A LITTLE STIFF, GIRLS! YOU MUST LOOSEN YOUR ARMS...
TOOM TOO TOOM
TOO TOOM
TOOM TOO TOOM
...AND ESPECIALLY FREE UP YOUR HEAD!
TOOM TOO TOOM
IT MUST FOLLOW YOUR BODY'S MOVEMENTS!
TOOM TOO TOOM
NOW YOU'RE GETTING IT!
TOOM TOO TOOM TOOM TOO TOOM
TOOM
THAT'S GOOD, GIRLS!
I CAN REALLY TELL YOU GAVE YOUR ALL!
THAT'S WHY WE'RE STOPPING EARLY!
YOU'LL NEED A GOOD TEN MINUTES TO UNTANGLE YOUR HAIR!
?
?
?
?
?

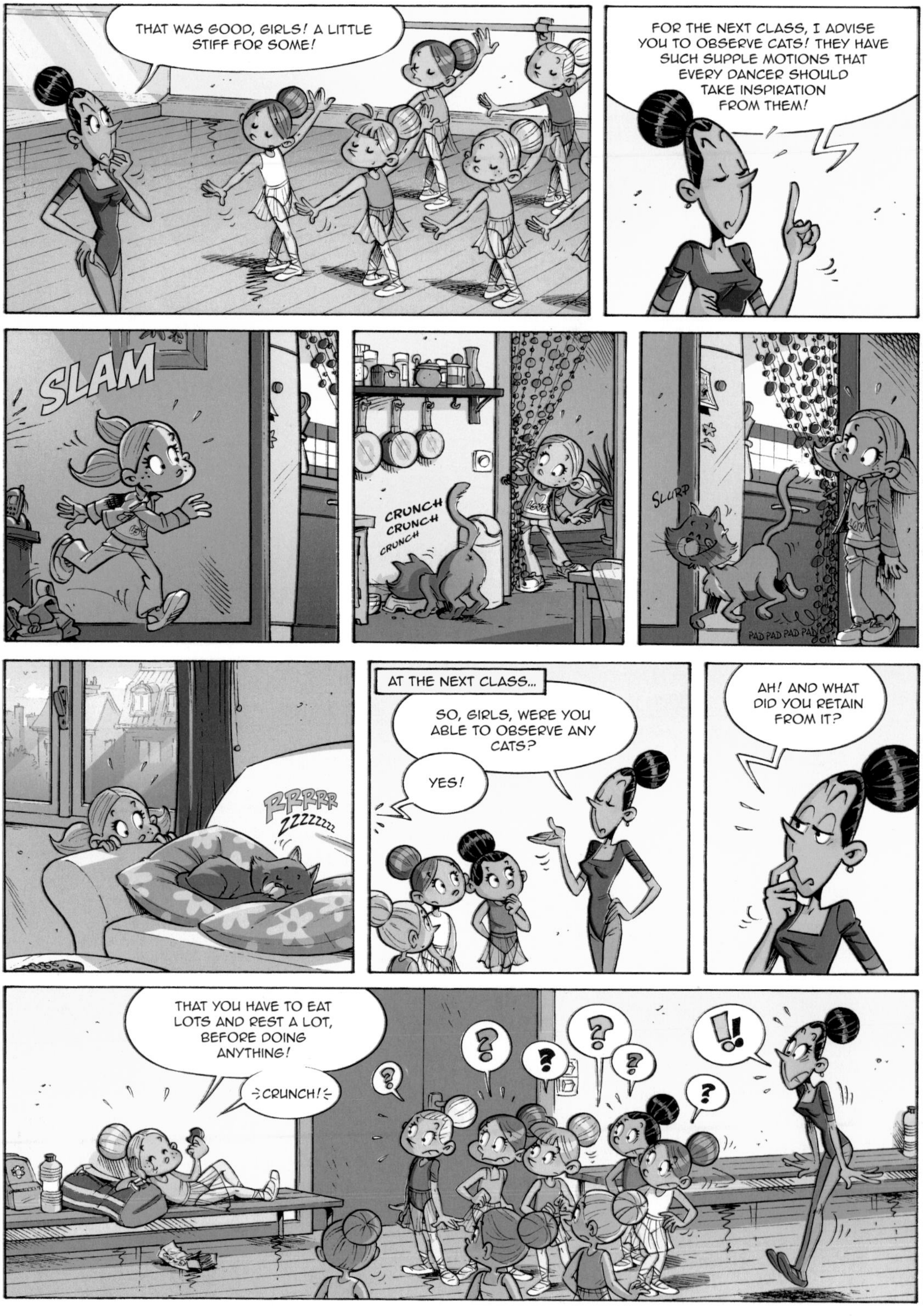
THAT WAS GOOD, GIRLS! A LITTLE STIFF FOR SOME!
FOR THE NEXT CLASS, I ADVISE YOU TO OBSERVE CATS! THEY HAVE SUCH SUPPLE MOTIONS THAT EVERY DANCER SHOULD TAKE INSPIRATION FROM THEM!
SLAM
CRUNCH CRUNCH CRUNCH
SLURP
PAD PAD PAD PAD
RRRRR ZZZZZZZ
AT THE NEXT CLASS...
SO, GIRLS, WERE YOU ABLE TO OBSERVE ANY CATS?
YES!
AH! AND WHAT DID YOU RETAIN FROM IT?
THAT YOU HAVE TO EAT LOTS AND REST A LOT, BEFORE DOING ANYTHING!
CRUNCH!
?
?
?
?
?
?
!!

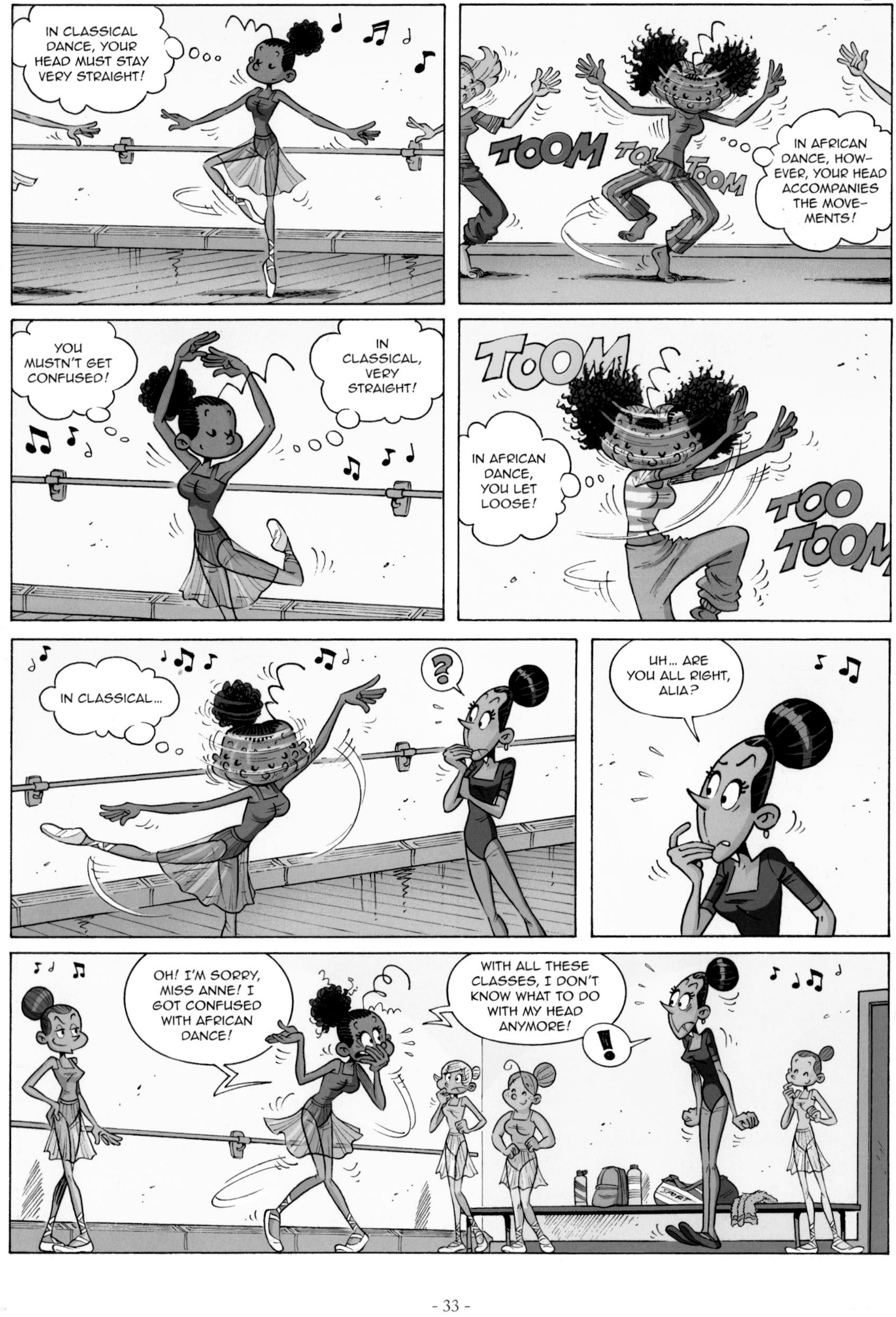
IN CLASSICAL DANCE, YOUR HEAD MUST STAY VERY STRAIGHT!
TOOM TOI TOOM
IN AFRICAN DANCE, HOW-EVER, YOUR HEAD ACCOMPANIES THE MOVE-MENTS!
YOU MUSTN'T GET CONFUSED!
IN CLASSICAL, VERY STRAIGHT!
TOOM
IN AFRICAN DANCE, YOU LET LOOSE!
TOO TOOM
IN CLASSICAL...
?
UH... ARE YOU ALL RIGHT, ALIA?
OH! I'M SORRY, MISS ANNE! I GOT CONFUSED WITH AFRICAN DANCE!
WITH ALL THESE CLASSES, I DON'T KNOW WHAT TO DO WITH MY HEAD ANYMORE!
!

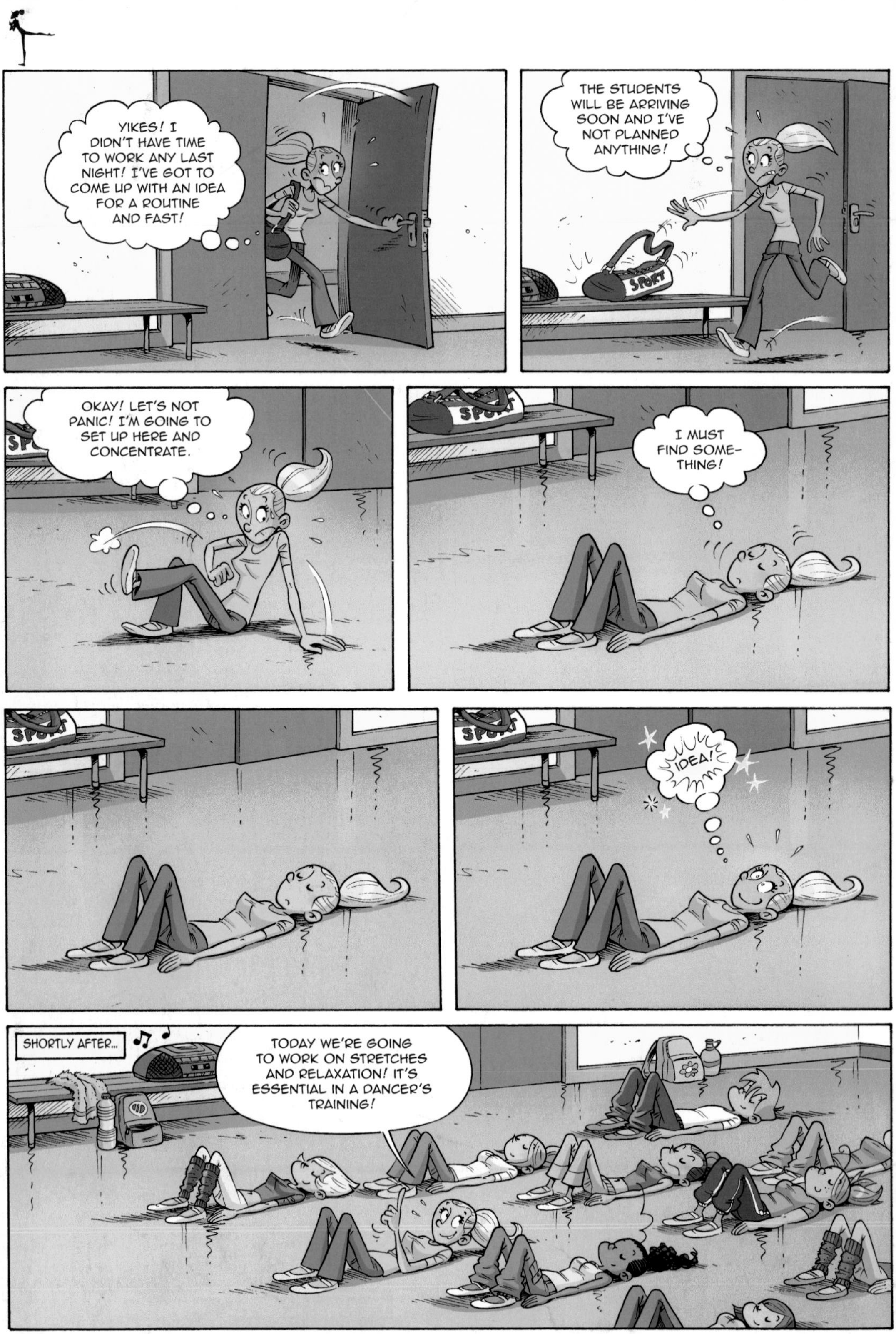
YIKES! I DIDN'T HAVE TIME TO WORK ANY LAST NIGHT! I'VE GOT TO COME UP WITH AN IDEA FOR A ROUTINE AND FAST!
THE STUDENTS WILL BE ARRIVING SOON AND I'VE NOT PLANNED ANYTHING!
SPORT
OKAY! LET'S NOT PANIC! I'M GOING TO SET UP HERE AND CONCENTRATE.
I MUST FIND SOME-THING!
IDEA!
SHORTLY AFTER...
TODAY WE'RE GOING TO WORK ON STRETCHES AND RELAXATION! IT'S ESSENTIAL IN A DANCER'S TRAINING!

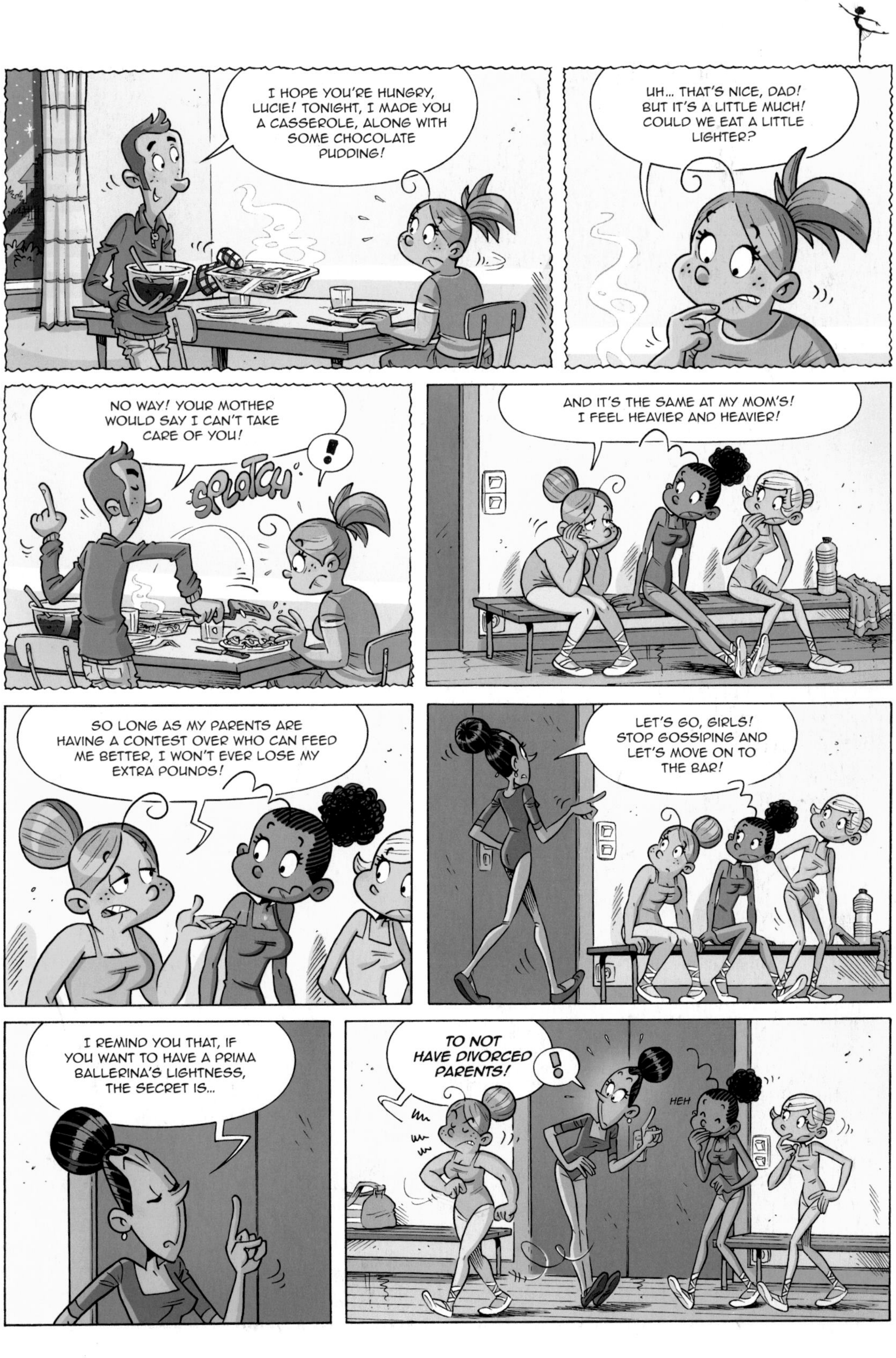

I HOPE YOU'RE HUNGRY, LUCIE! TONIGHT, I MADE YOU A CASSEROLE, ALONG WITH SOME CHOCOLATE PUDDING!
UH... THAT'S NICE, DAD! BUT IT'S A LITTLE MUCH! COULD WE EAT A LITTLE LIGHTER?
NO WAY! YOUR MOTHER WOULD SAY I CAN'T TAKE CARE OF YOU!
SPLOTCH
!
AND IT'S THE SAME AT MY MOM'S! I FEEL HEAVIER AND HEAVIER!
SO LONG AS MY PARENTS ARE HAVING A CONTEST OVER WHO CAN FEED ME BETTER, I WON'T EVER LOSE MY EXTRA POUNDS!
LET'S GO, GIRLS! STOP GOSSIPING AND LET'S MOVE ON TO THE BAR!
I REMIND YOU THAT, IF YOU WANT TO HAVE A PRIMA BALLERINA'S LIGHTNESS, THE SECRET IS...
TO NOT HAVE DIVORCED PARENTS!
!
HEH

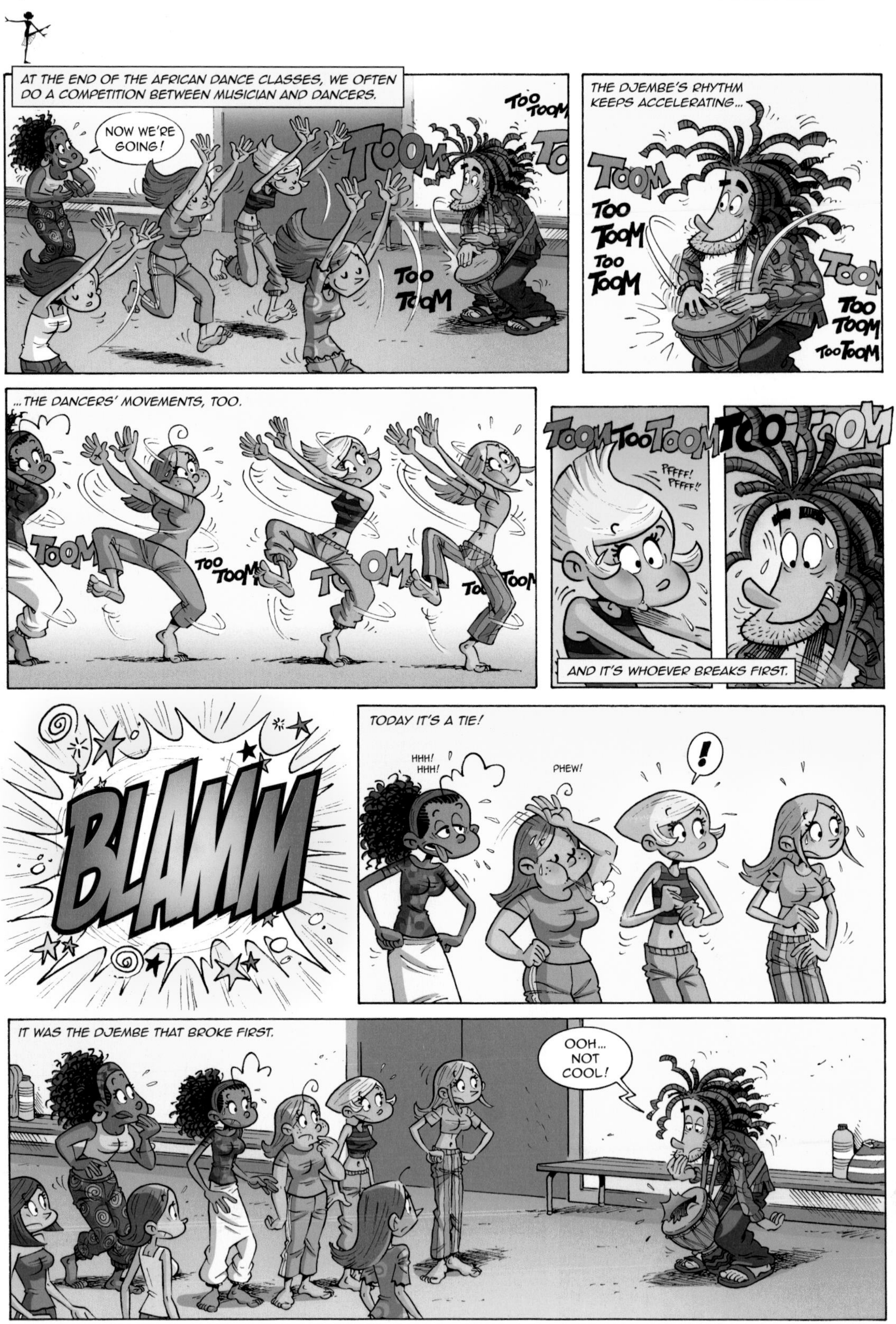

AT THE END OF THE AFRICAN DANCE CLASSES, WE OFTEN DO A COMPETITION BETWEEN MUSICIAN AND DANCERS.
NOW WE'RE GOING!
TOOM
TOO TOOM
TOO TOOM
THE DJEMBE'S RHYTHM KEEPS ACCELERATING...
TOOM
TOO TOOM
TOO TOOM
TOO TOOM
TOO TOOM
...THE DANCERS' MOVEMENTS, TOO.
TOOM
TOO TOOM
TOOM
TOO TOOM
TOOM TOO TOOM TOO TOOM
PFFFF! PFFFF!!
AND IT'S WHOEVER BREAKS FIRST.
BLAMM
TODAY IT'S A TIE!
HHH! HHH!
PHEW!
!
IT WAS THE DJEMBE THAT BROKE FIRST.
OOH... NOT COOL!

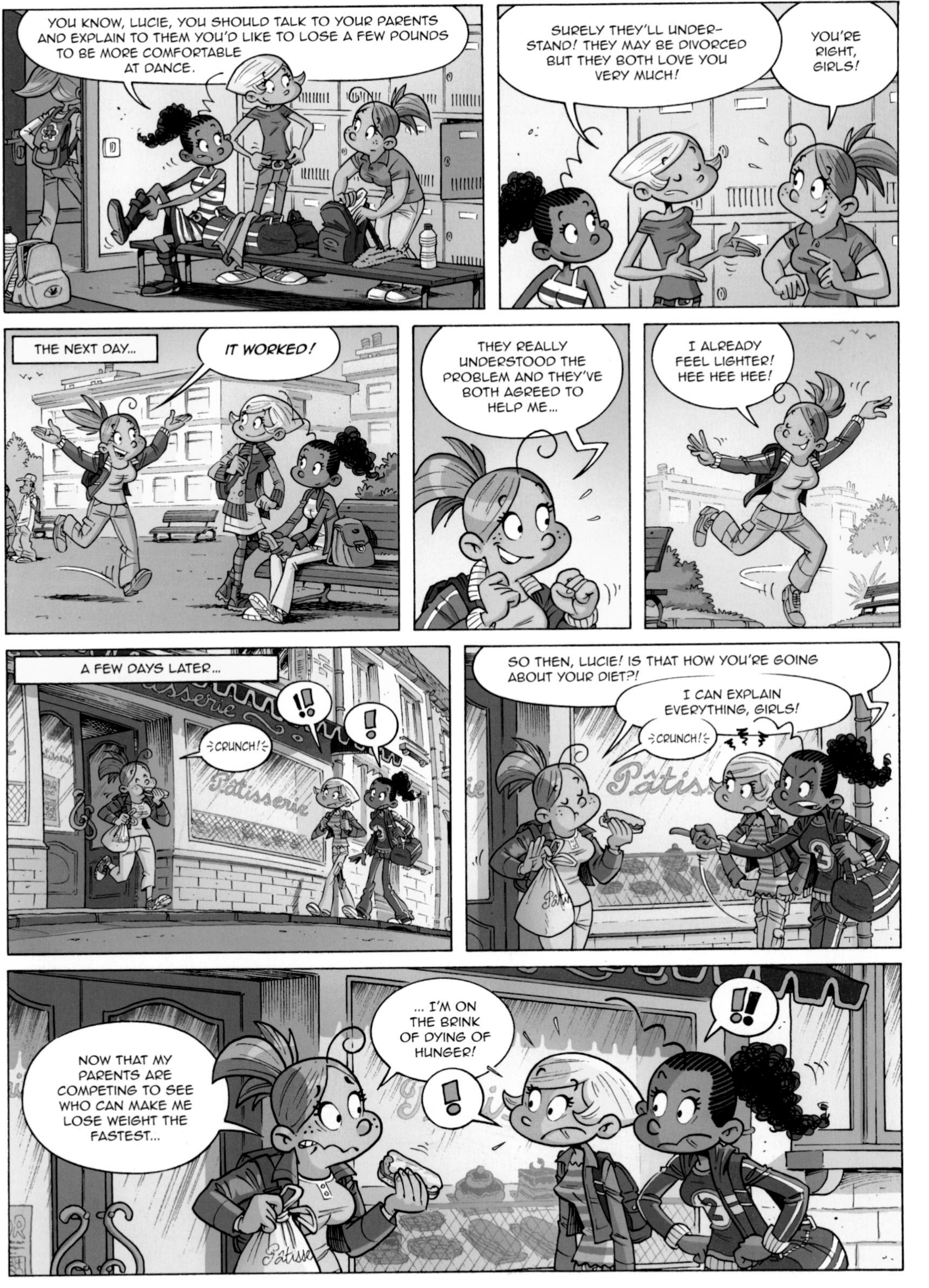
YOU KNOW, LUCIE, YOU SHOULD TALK TO YOUR PARENTS AND EXPLAIN TO THEM YOU'D LIKE TO LOSE A FEW POUNDS TO BE MORE COMFORTABLE AT DANCE.
SURELY THEY'LL UNDER-STAND! THEY MAY BE DIVORCED BUT THEY BOTH LOVE YOU VERY MUCH!
YOU'RE RIGHT, GIRLS!
THE NEXT DAY...
IT WORKED!
THEY REALLY UNDERSTOOD THE PROBLEM AND THEY'VE BOTH AGREED TO HELP ME...
I ALREADY FEEL LIGHTER! HEE HEE HEE!
A FEW DAYS LATER...
CRUNCH!
!!
!
SO THEN, LUCIE! IS THAT HOW YOU'RE GOING ABOUT YOUR DIET?!
I CAN EXPLAIN EVERYTHING, GIRLS!
CRUNCH!
NOW THAT MY PARENTS ARE COMPETING TO SEE WHO CAN MAKE ME LOSE WEIGHT THE FASTEST...
... I'M ON THE BRINK OF DYING OF HUNGER!
!
!!

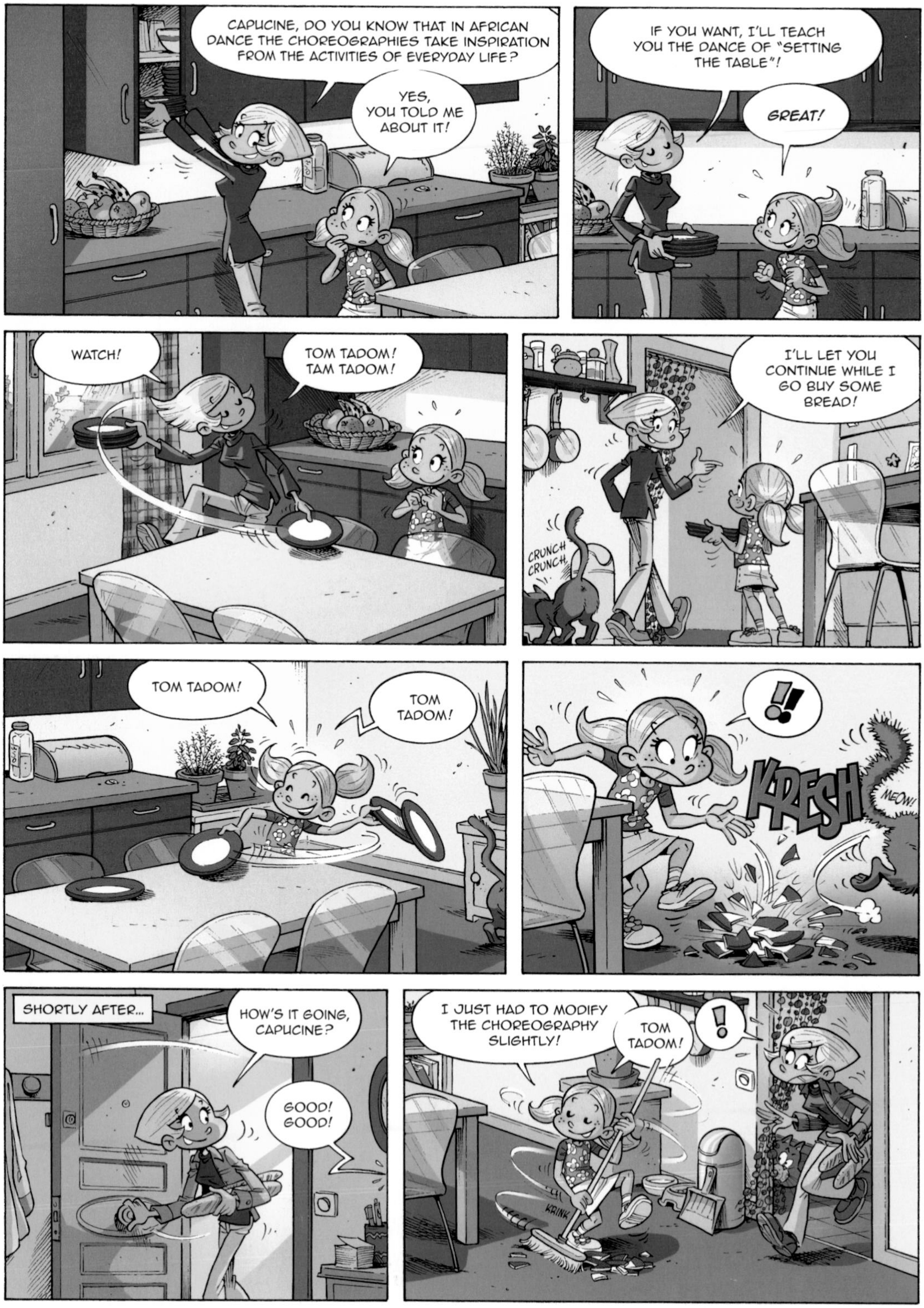

CAPUCINE, DO YOU KNOW THAT IN AFRICAN DANCE THE CHOREOGRAPHIES TAKE INSPIRATION FROM THE ACTIVITIES OF EVERYDAY LIFE?
YES, YOU TOLD ME ABOUT IT!
IF YOU WANT, I'LL TEACH YOU THE DANCE OF "SETTING THE TABLE"!
GREAT!
WATCH!
TOM TADOM! TAM TADOM!
I'LL LET YOU CONTINUE WHILE I GO BUY SOME BREAD!
CRUNCH CRUNCH
TOM TADOM!
TOM TADOM!
!!
KRESH
MEOW!
SHORTLY AFTER...
HOW'S IT GOING, CAPUCINE?
GOOD! GOOD!
I JUST HAD TO MODIFY THE CHOREOGRAPHY SLIGHTLY!
TOM TADOM!
!
KRINK

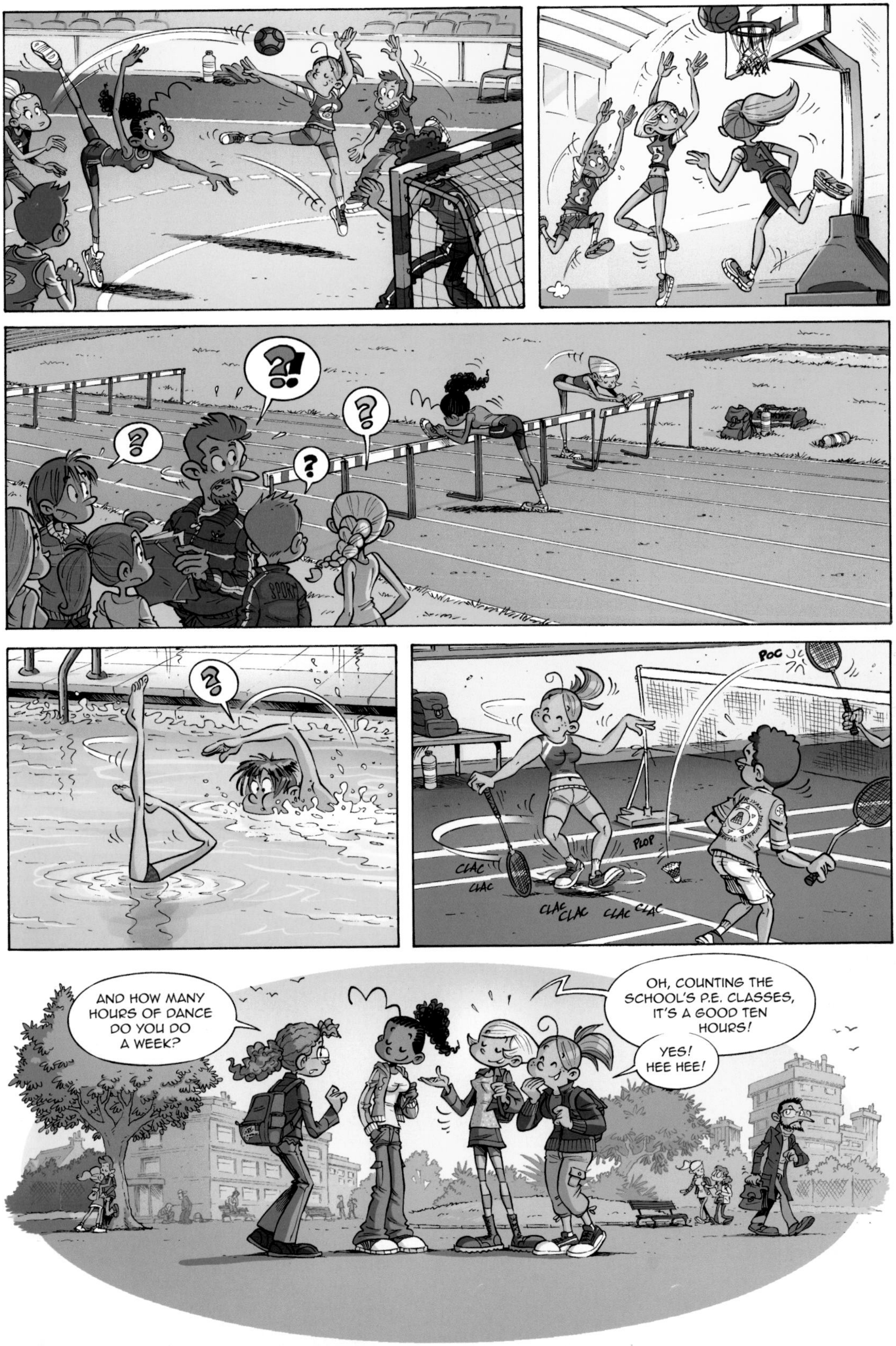

?!
?
?
?
?
POC
PLOP
CLAC
CLAC
CLAC CLAC CLAC CLAC
AND HOW MANY HOURS OF DANCE DO YOU DO A WEEK?
OH, COUNTING THE SCHOOL'S P.E. CLASSES, IT'S A GOOD TEN HOURS!
YES! HEE HEE!

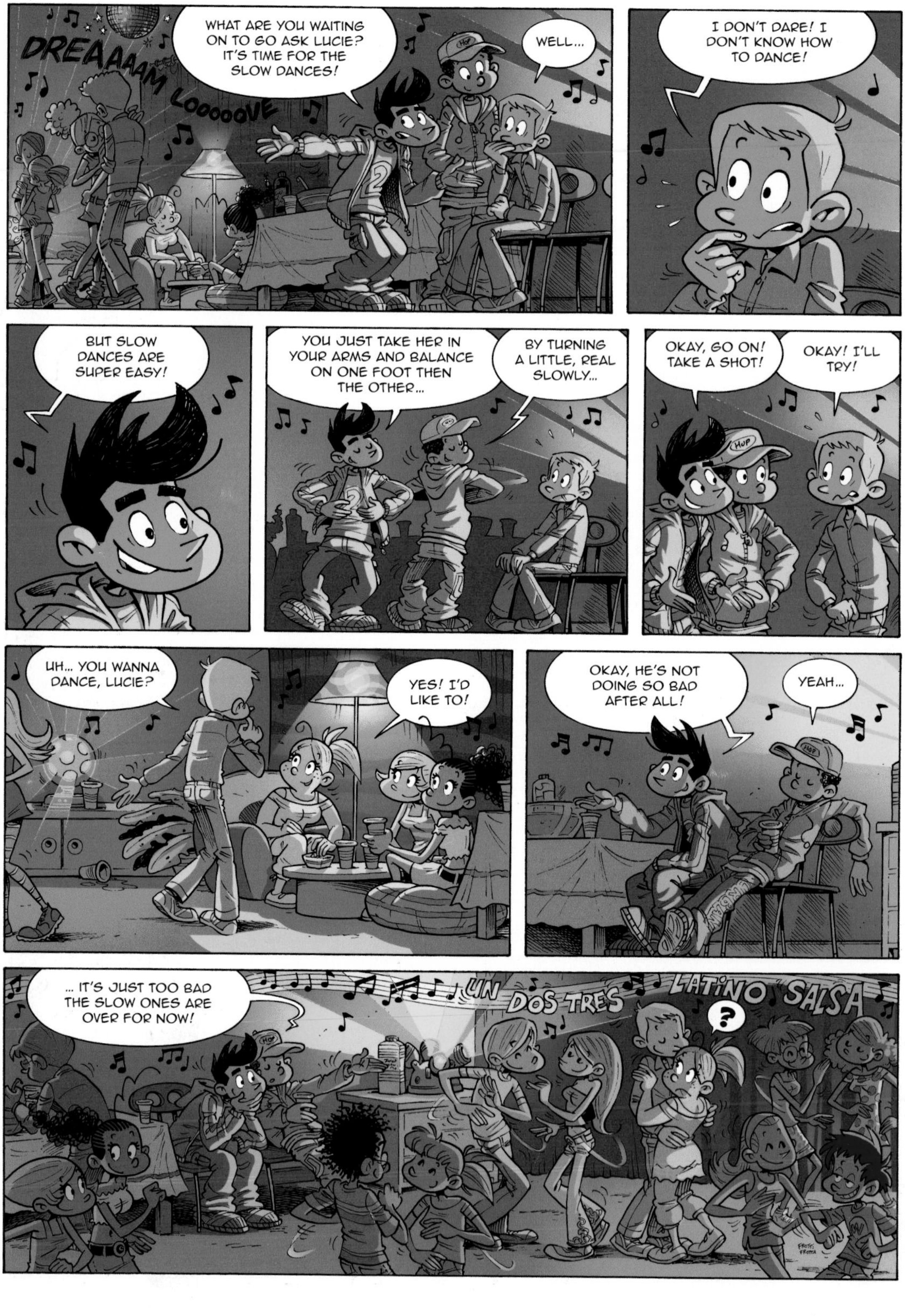
DREAAAAM LOOOOOVE
WHAT ARE YOU WAITING ON TO GO ASK LUCIE? IT'S TIME FOR THE SLOW DANCES!
WELL...
I DON'T DARE! I DON'T KNOW HOW TO DANCE!
BUT SLOW DANCES ARE SUPER EASY!
YOU JUST TAKE HER IN YOUR ARMS AND BALANCE ON ONE FOOT THEN THE OTHER...
BY TURNING A LITTLE, REAL SLOWLY...
OKAY, GO ON! TAKE A SHOT!
OKAY! I'LL TRY!
UH... YOU WANNA DANCE, LUCIE?
YES! I'D LIKE TO!
OKAY, HE'S NOT DOING SO BAD AFTER ALL!
YEAH...
... IT'S JUST TOO BAD THE SLOW ONES ARE OVER FOR NOW!
UN DOS TRES LATINO SALSA
?

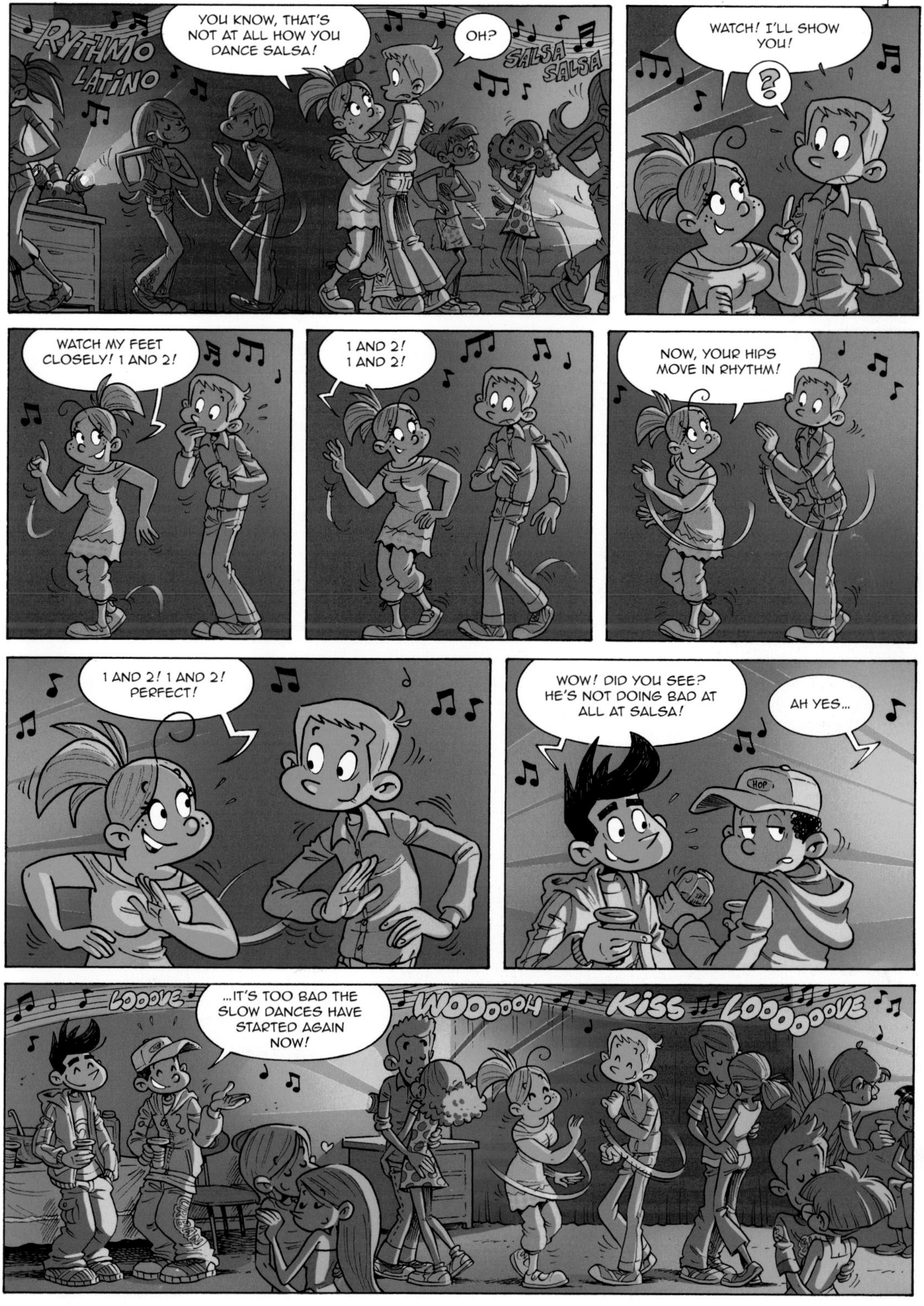

RYTHMO LATINO
YOU KNOW, THAT'S NOT AT ALL HOW YOU DANCE SALSA!
OH?
SALSA SALSA
WATCH! I'LL SHOW YOU!
?
WATCH MY FEET CLOSELY! 1 AND 2!
1 AND 2! 1 AND 2!
NOW, YOUR HIPS MOVE IN RHYTHM!
1 AND 2! 1 AND 2! PERFECT!
WOW! DID YOU SEE? HE'S NOT DOING BAD AT ALL AT SALSA!
AH YES...
HOP
LOOOVE
...IT'S TOO BAD THE SLOW DANCES HAVE STARTED AGAIN NOW!
WOOooOH
KISS
LOOOOOOVE

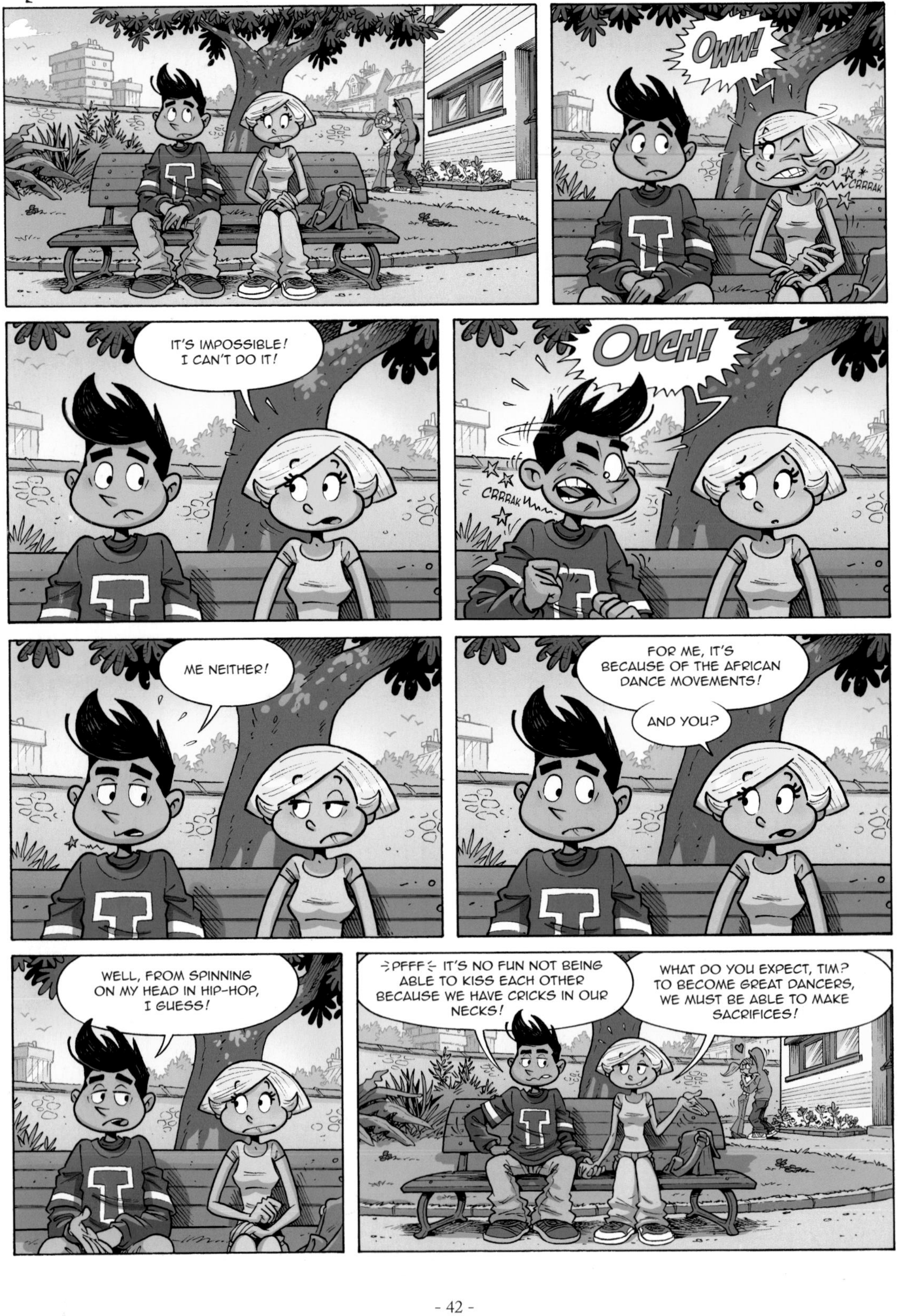
OWW!
CRRRAK
IT'S IMPOSSIBLE! I CAN'T DO IT!
OUCH!
CRRRAK
ME NEITHER!
FOR ME, IT'S BECAUSE OF THE AFRICAN DANCE MOVEMENTS!
AND YOU?
WELL, FROM SPINNING ON MY HEAD IN HIP-HOP, I GUESS!
PFFF IT'S NO FUN NOT BEING ABLE TO KISS EACH OTHER BECAUSE WE HAVE CRICKS IN OUR NECKS!
WHAT DO YOU EXPECT, TIM? TO BECOME GREAT DANCERS, WE MUST BE ABLE TO MAKE SACRIFICES!

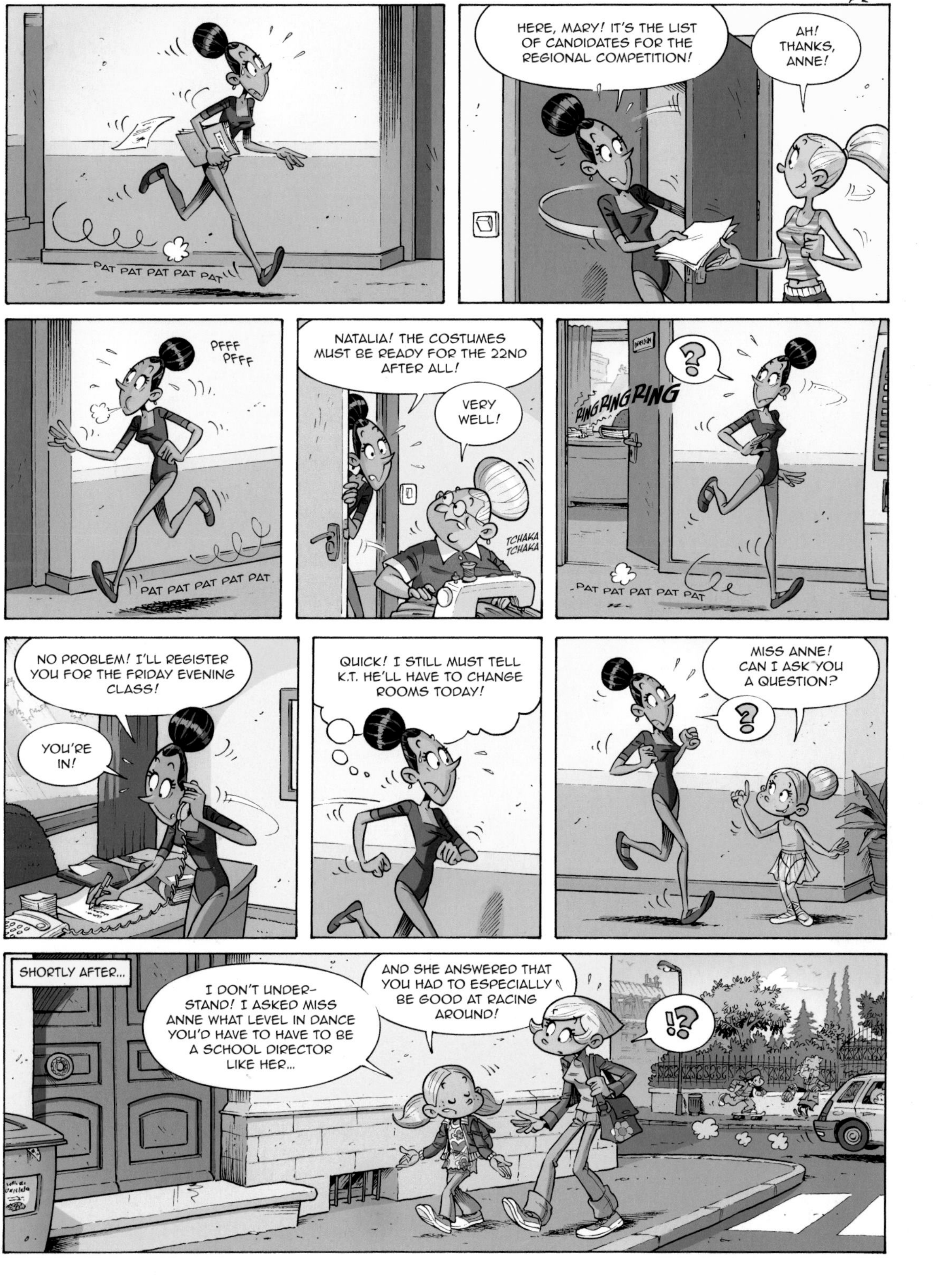
PAT PAT PAT PAT PAT
HERE, MARY! IT'S THE LIST OF CANDIDATES FOR THE REGIONAL COMPETITION!
AH! THANKS, ANNE!
PFFF PFFF
PAT PAT PAT PAT PAT
NATALIA! THE COSTUMES MUST BE READY FOR THE 22ND AFTER ALL!
VERY WELL!
TCHAKA TCHAKA
?
RING RING RING
PAT PAT PAT PAT PAT
NO PROBLEM! I'LL REGISTER YOU FOR THE FRIDAY EVENING CLASS!
YOU'RE IN!
QUICK! I STILL MUST TELL K.T. HE'LL HAVE TO CHANGE ROOMS TODAY!
MISS ANNE! CAN I ASK YOU A QUESTION?
?
SHORTLY AFTER...
I DON'T UNDERSTAND! I ASKED MISS ANNE WHAT LEVEL IN DANCE YOU'D HAVE TO HAVE TO BE A SCHOOL DIRECTOR LIKE HER...
AND SHE ANSWERED THAT YOU HAD TO ESPECIALLY BE GOOD AT RACING AROUND!
!?

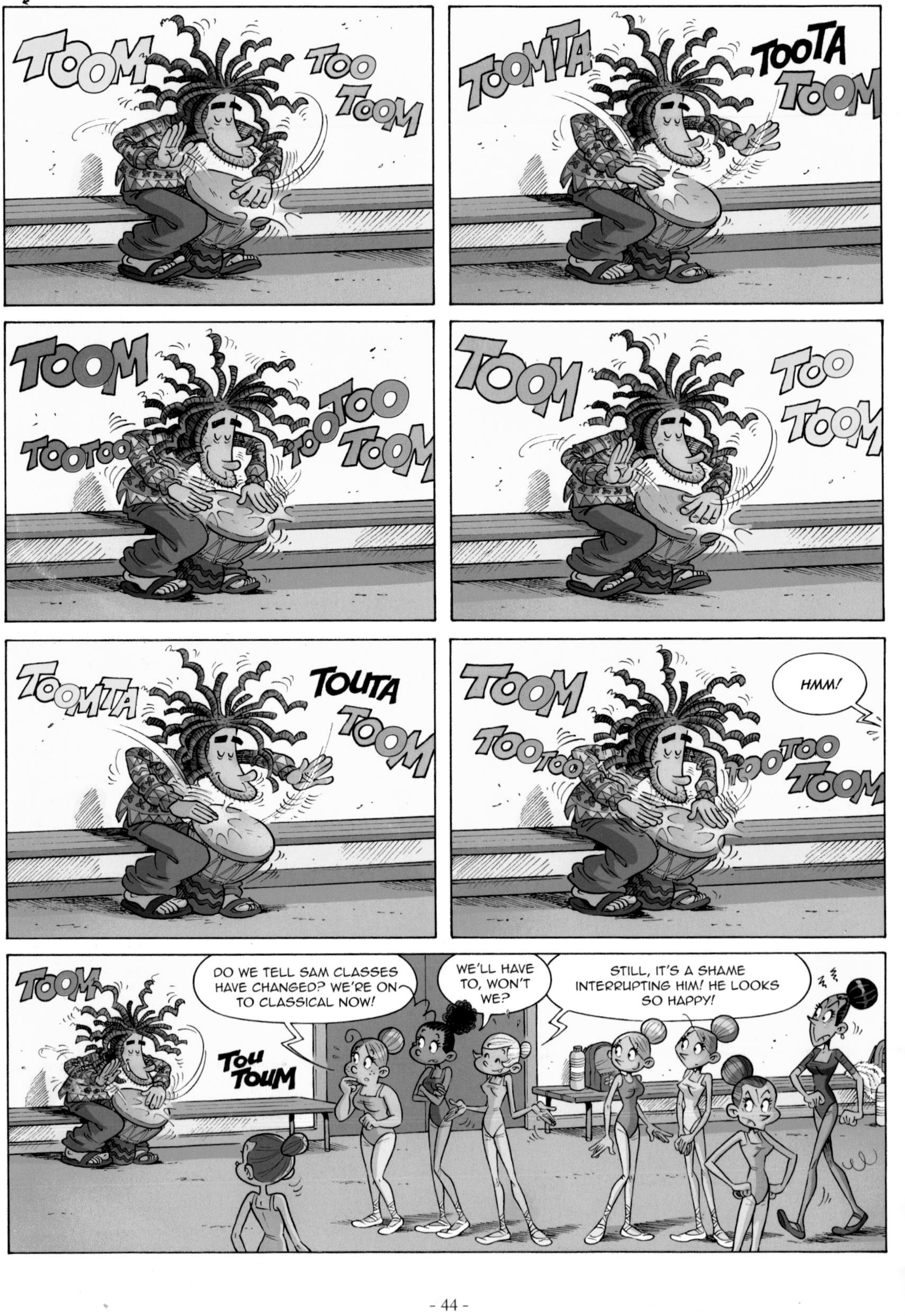
TOOM
TOO TOOM
TOOMTA
TOOTA TOOM
TOOM
TOOTOO
TOOTOO TOOM
TOOM
TOO TOOM
TOOMTA
TOUTA TOOM
TOOM
TOOTOO
HMM!
TOOTOO TOOM
TOOM
DO WE TELL SAM CLASSES HAVE CHANGED? WE'RE ON TO CLASSICAL NOW!
TOU TOUM
WE'LL HAVE TO, WON'T WE?
STILL, IT'S A SHAME INTERRUPTING HIM! HE LOOKS SO HAPPY!

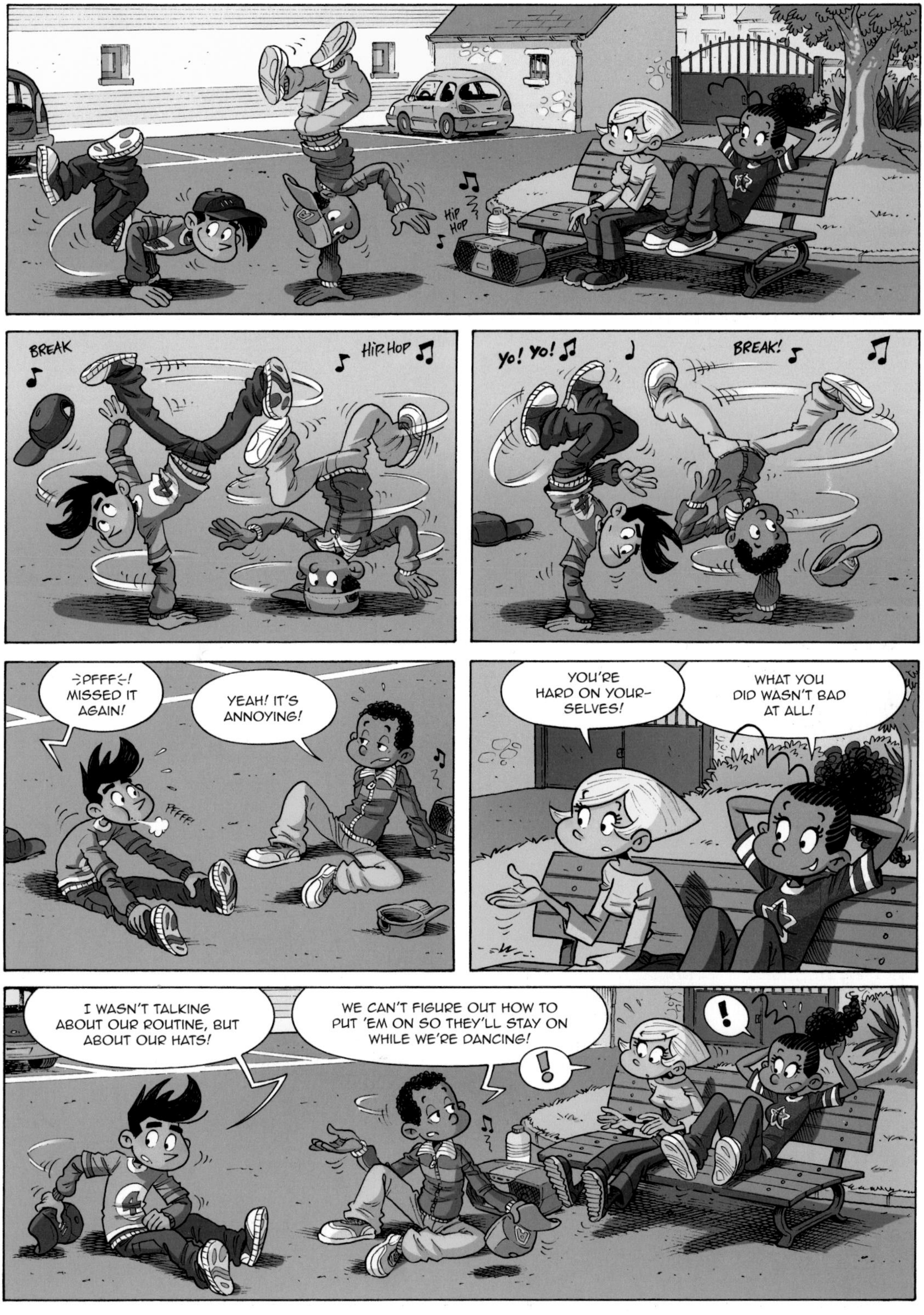
Hip Hop
BREAK
Hip Hop
Yo! Yo!
BREAK!
PFFF!
MISSED IT AGAIN!
YEAH! IT'S ANNOYING!
PFFF!
YOU'RE HARD ON YOURSELVES!
WHAT YOU DID WASN'T BAD AT ALL!
I WASN'T TALKING ABOUT OUR ROUTINE, BUT ABOUT OUR HATS!
WE CAN'T FIGURE OUT HOW TO PUT 'EM ON SO THEY'LL STAY ON WHILE WE'RE DANCING!
!
!

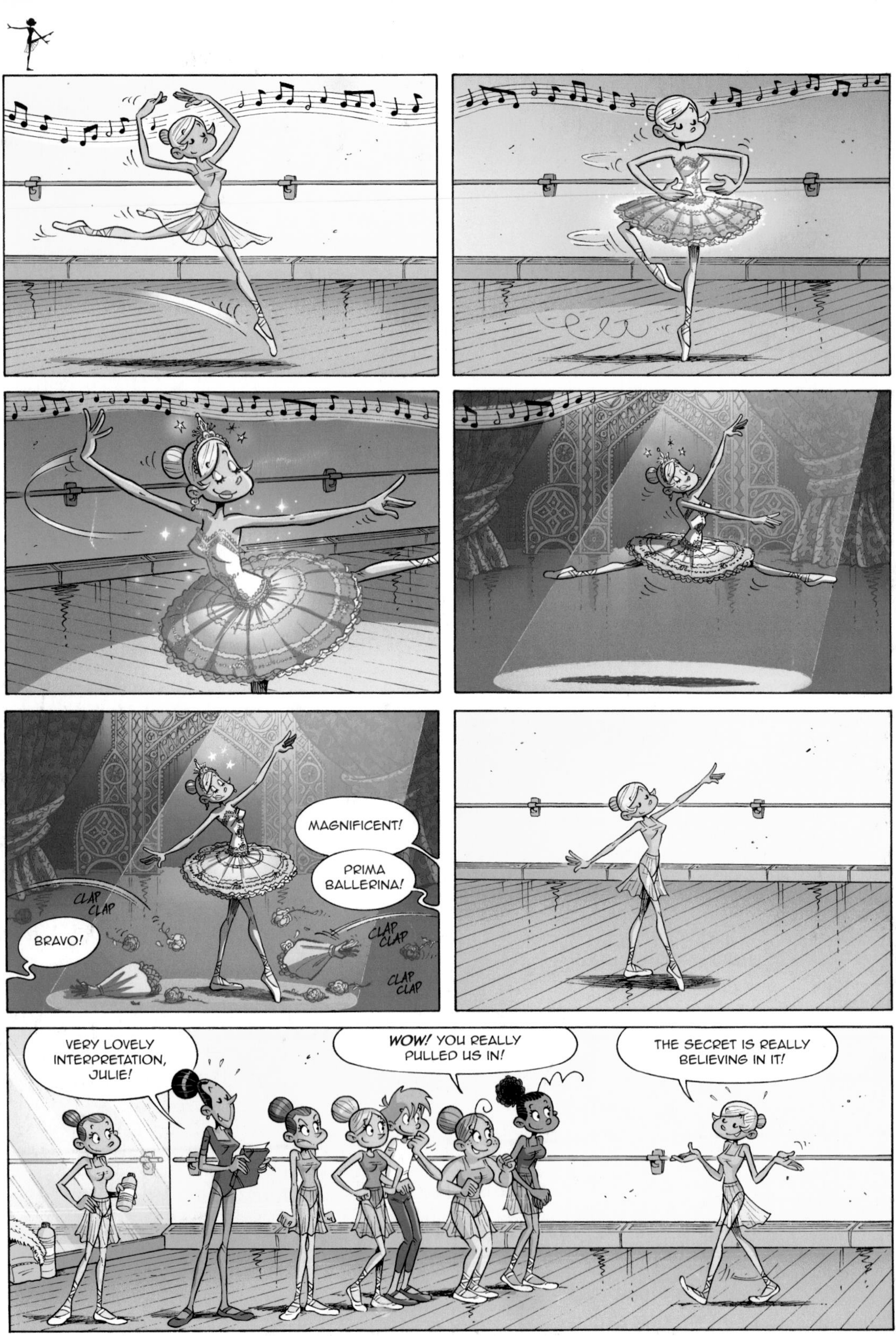

MAGNIFICENT!
PRIMA BALLERINA!
CLAP CLAP
BRAVO!
CLAP CLAP
CLAP CLAP
VERY LOVELY INTERPRETATION, JULIE!
WOW! YOU REALLY PULLED US IN!
THE SECRET IS REALLY BELIEVING IN IT!

WATCH OUT FOR PAPERCUTZ™

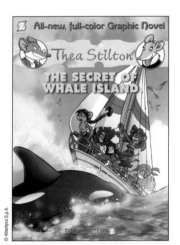
All-new, full-color Graphic Novel
Thea Stilton
THE SECRET OF WHALE ISLAND

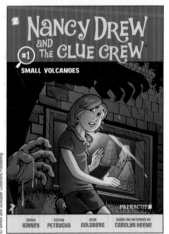
NANCY DREW AND THE CLUE CREW
#1
SMALL VOLCANOES
SARAH KINNEY · STEFAN PETRUCHA · SEAN GOLDBERG · BASED ON THE SERIES BY CAROLYN KEENE
PAPERCUTZ

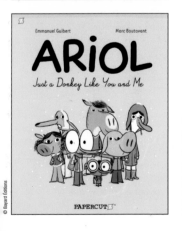
Emmanuel Guibert · Marc Boutavant
ARIOL
Just a Donkey Like You and Me
PAPERCUTZ

Welcome to the toe-tapping third DANCE CLASS graphic novel by Crip & Béka. I'm Jim Salicrup, your tutu-wearing Editor-in-Chief of Papercutz, the dance-challenged folks who are dedicated to publishing great graphic novels for all ages. I'm here to let you know a little about what goes on behind-the-scenes here at Papercutz, but the very best way to find out what's new and exciting at Papercutz is to check out our new and improved web-site.

Here's a quick story. Shortly after DANCE CLASS #1 "So You Think You Can Hip-Hop" was published, I attended an off-Broadway play that featured my multi-talented dance teacher, Liz Peterson, in a role. After the show, I proudly presented her with a copy of DANCE CLASS #1, which mentioned her as one of my dance teachers. While Liz was happy and thankful to get the graphic novel, one of her awesomely talented friends, a woman named Pepper, was very interested in the book too! Turns out as a choreographer, she's very involved in fusing elements of hip-hop with classical dance—so you can see why she was intrigued by the title. While DANCE CLASS is mostly a light-hearted series focusing on the lives of several young girls studying dance, it's nice to know it can still capture the eye of such talented and artistic dancers.

And speaking of capturing your eye, Papercutz is launching a bunch of new graphic novel series that may just be of interest to you!

First is THEA STILTON. Yes, that's the name of Geronimo Stilton's adventurous sister, but this series is all about The Thea Sisters at Mouseford Academy on Whale Island. The premiere volume is "The Secret of Whale Island."

And speaking of light-hearted series featuring girls, NANCY DREW AND THE CLUE CREW should be available now at booksellers everywhere. Unlike her previous Papercutz series, Nancy is just eight-years old in this one! But that's not keeping her from solving mysteries, with her besties George and Bess, at River Heights Elementary School! The first volume is entitled "Small Volcanoes." Interesting—Papercutz provides quite an age range of female characters! From six and a half year old Rebecca in ERNEST & REBECCA, to the pre-teens in NANCY DREW AND THE CLUE CREW, to the teens in DANCE CLASS, to the college students in THEA STILTON!

And finally, there's ARIOL! It's a new series from multiple award-winning author Emmanuel Guibert and renowned illustrator Marc Boutavant. Unlike the girls we were just talking about, who were mostly human (THEA STILTON features mice!), Ariol is your everyday tween donkey with big blue glasses. His best friend is a pig. He's in love with a cow in his class. His teacher is a dog. His gym teacher a rooster. In short, he's just like you and me. Don't miss ARIOL #1 "Just a Donkey Like You and Me."

For previews of all of the above, be sure to go to the Papercutz website! So, until DANCE CLASS #4 "A Funny Thing Happened on the Way to Paris," keep on dancin'!

STAY IN TOUCH!

EMAIL: salicrup@papercutz.com
WEB: www.papercutz.com
TWITTER: @papercutzgn
FACEBOOK: PAPERCUTZGRAPHICNOVELS
BIRTHDAY CARDS: Papercutz, 160 Broadway,
Suite 700, East Wing, New York, NY 10038

Thanks,

Jim

Caricature drawn by Steve Brodner at the MoCCA Art Fest

More Great Graphic Novels from PAPERCUTZ

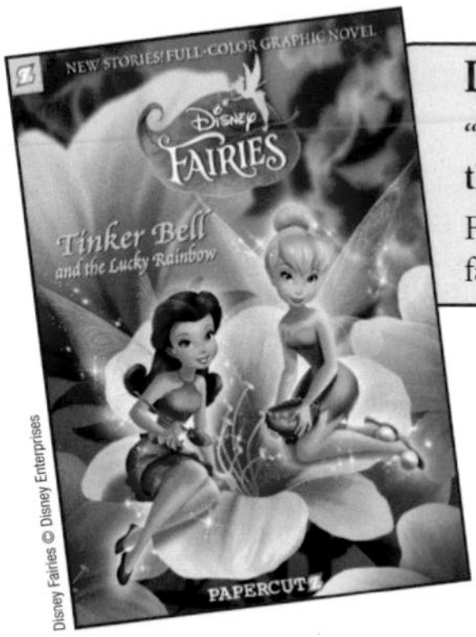

NEW STORIES! FULL-COLOR GRAPHIC NOVEL
Disney FAIRIES
Tinker Bell and the Lucky Rainbow
PAPERCUTZ

DISNEY FAIRIES #10

"Tinker Bell and the Lucky Rainbow"

Four magical tales featuring the fairies from Pixie Hollow!

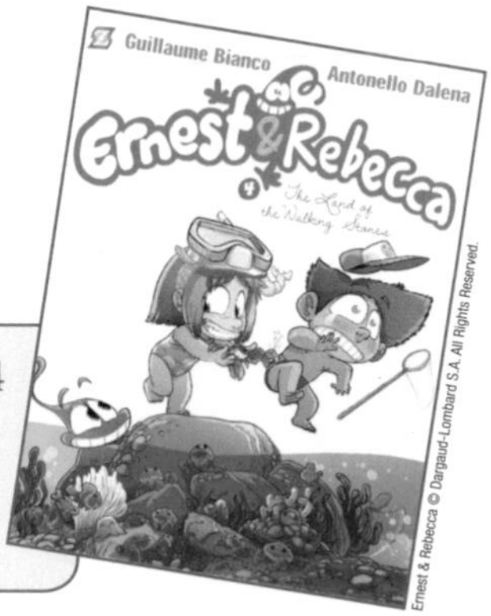

Guillaume Bianco
Antonello Dalena
Ernest & Rebecca

ERNEST & REBECCA #4

"The Land of Walking Stones"

A 6 ½ year old girl and her microbial buddy against the world!

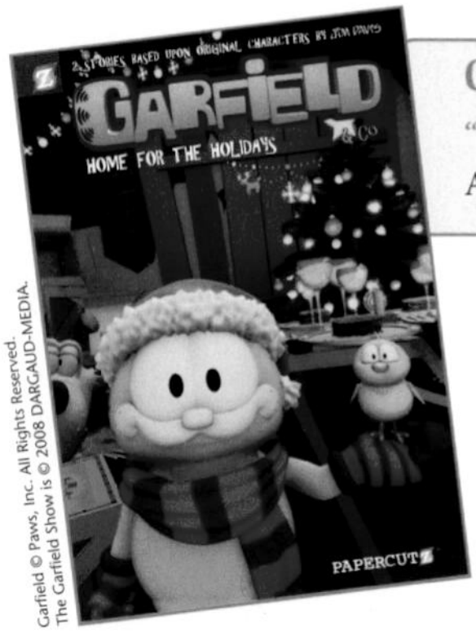

GARFIELD
HOME FOR THE HOLIDAYS
PAPERCUTZ

GARFIELD & Co #7

"Home for the Holidays"

As seen on the Cartoon Network!

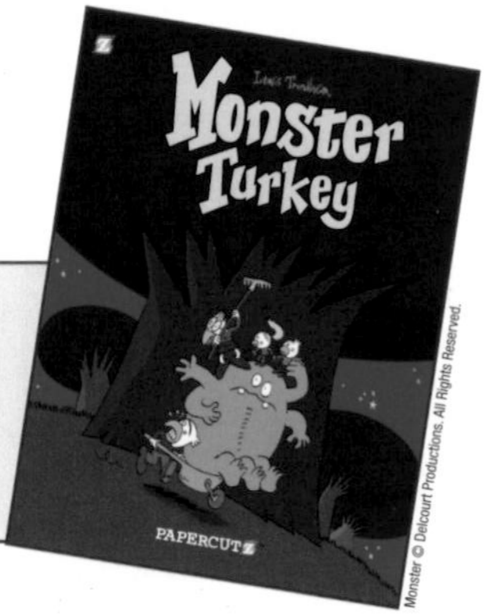

Monster Turkey
PAPERCUTZ

MONSTER #4

"Monster Turkey"

The almost normal adventures of an almost ordinary family... with a pet monster!

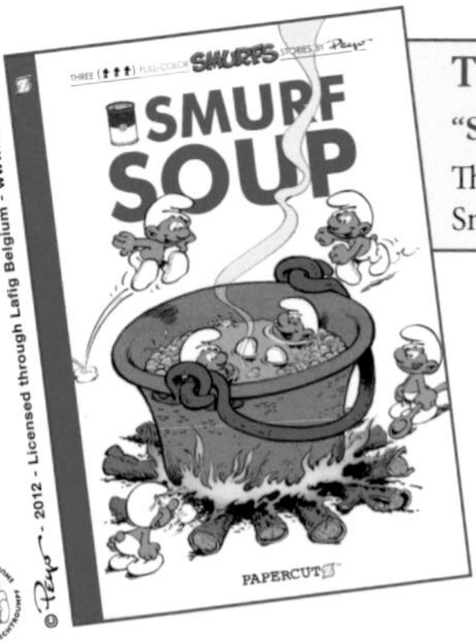

SMURFS
SMURF SOUP
PAPERCUTZ

THE SMURFS #13

"Smurf Soup"

There's big trouble brewing in the Smurfs Village!

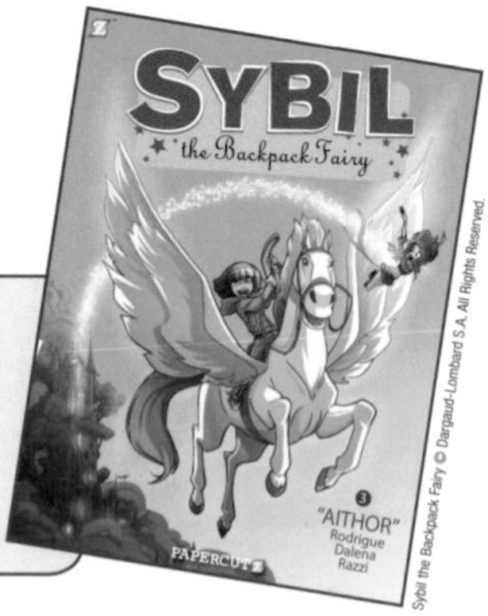

SYBIL
the Backpack Fairy
3
"AITHOR"
Rodrigue
Dalena
Razzi
PAPERCUTZ

SYBIL THE BACKPACK FAIRY #3

"Aithor"

What's cooler than a fairy in your backpack? How about a flying horse?!

Available at better booksellers everywhere!

Or order directly from us! DISNEY FAIRIES is available in paperback for $7.99, in hardcover for $11.99; ERNEST & REBECCA is $11.99 in hardcover only; GARFIELD & Co is available in hardcover only for $7.99; MONSTER is available in hardcover only for $9.99; THE SMURFS are available in paperback for $5.99, in hardcover for $10.99; and SYBIL THE BACKPACK FAIRY is available in hardcover only for $11.99.

Please add $4.00 for postage and handling for the first book, add $1.00 for each additional book.

Please make check payable to NBM Publishing. Send to: PAPERCUTZ, 160 Broadway, Suite 700, East Wing, New York, NY 10038
Or call 800-886-1223, 9AM-6PM EST, M-F

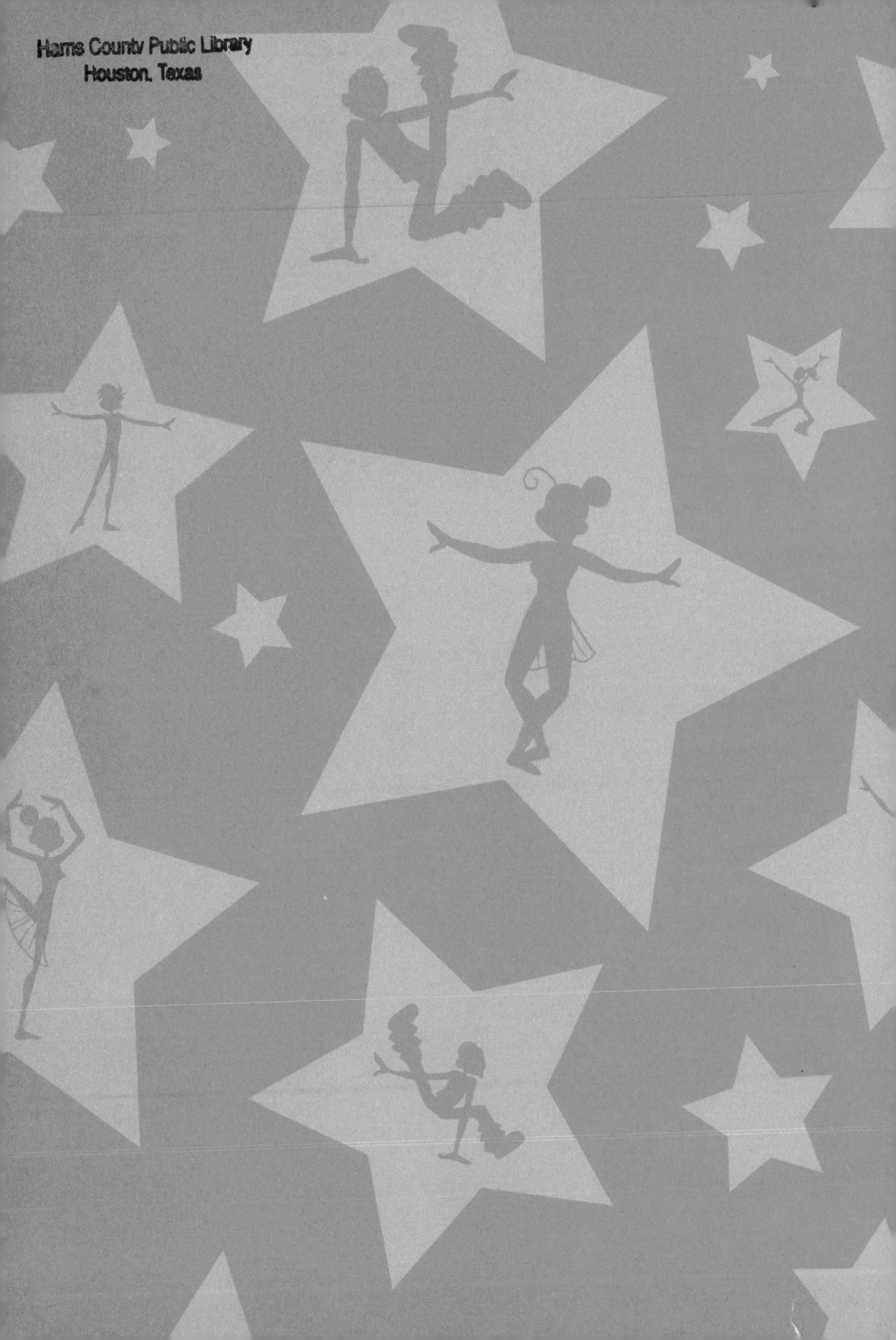